HANGMAN'S COUNTRY

**Center Point
Large Print**

**This Large Print Book carries the
Seal of Approval of N.A.V.H.**

HANGMAN'S COUNTRY

LEWIS B. PATTEN

CENTER POINT PUBLISHING
THORNDIKE, MAINE

This Center Point Large Print edition
is published in the year 2004 by arrangement with
Golden West Literary Agency.

The text of this Large Print edition is unabridged. In other
aspects, this book may vary from the original edition. Printed in
Thailand. Set in 16-point Times New Roman type.

ISBN 1-58547-453-3

Library of Congress Cataloging-in-Publication Data

Patten, Lewis B.
    Hangman's country / Lewis B. Patten.--Center Point large print ed.
        p. cm.
    ISBN 1-58547-453-3 (lib. bdg. : alk. paper)
        1. Large type books. I. Title.

PS3566.A79H36 2004
813'.54--dc22

                                                                2004000966

CHAPTER ONE

At sundown on the 7th of July, the year Stuart Post was twenty, Ken Ivy came spurring down the lane at Skull Ranch on a lathered, faltering horse.

He hauled up under the spread of a monstrous cottonwood that stood in the dusty yard, slid to the ground and crossed to the house at a stiff, fast walk.

From the open door of the blacksmith shop, where he was sweating over the forge, Stuart had watched him ride in. He turned back to his work, but minutes later he stopped again as his father's bull voice rolled out across the yard.

"Stu! Kill that forge and saddle up!"

Stuart cursed mildly, picked up a bucket of water that always stood beside the forge and dumped it over the glowing coals. A cloud of steam rolled to the ceiling, where it spread in all directions. Wiping his streaming forehead with a sleeve, Stu stepped from the door into the dying heat of the setting sun.

He was a tall young man, dark of hair and eye, with a spare, high-cheekboned face and a jutting, stubborn chin. His shoulders were broad and corded with rippling muscles, yet they had none of the ponderousness that characterized those of both his father, Milo, and his brother Ernie.

From his shoulders he tapered down to lean, dusty, jean-clad hips, which precariously supported a sagging gun and belt. His boots were run over at the heels, and his spurs left little trailing tracks in the dust as he walked.

He tipped back his hat and stared at Ken Ivy, who was now leading his horse across toward the corral. When Ken drew near, Stuart asked, "What's up?"

"It's that damn bunch down the creek. I found where one of 'em had pushed six steers through a cut fence and headed for Salt Wash."

"Could you tell who it was?"

Ivy shook his head. "Not by the tracks. But I saw Hugh Shore pokin' along under the rim yesterday morning. It was probably him."

Stuart felt a stir of concern. He hoped it wasn't Hugh. He hoped it was anyone but Hugh. He asked, "What's Milo going to do?"

"Ride to the cut fence tonight. Trail 'em as soon as it's light in the morning." Excitement shone in Ivy's eyes. He turned and led his horse on toward the corral. Stuart followed.

Uneasiness stirred in him, a vague kind of dread. This wasn't the first time one of the ranchers below Skull had helped himself to a few Skull cattle, but usually they were more careful. Whoever it was must have been desperate to risk doing it so openly.

Desperate. That word fitted most of the ranchers below Skull. In summer Skull took the whole of Colorow Creek to irrigate their vast hay meadows. Skull controlled all the rimrock trails leading to the high grass of the mesa top. The little ranches below them had only the cedar-covered benches below the rim on which to graze their cattle, hay that depended on what little flood water they could get in the spring, and a mortgage at the Sapovanero Bank.

Scowling, Stuart roped a horse out of the bunch in the corral, slipped a bridle over his head and flung a saddle onto his back. He tied the horse to the poles and roped another. He had three saddles by the time Milo and Ernie Post came striding arrogantly across the yard.

They were massive, top-heavy men with thick muscular shoulders and deep, strong chests. Both weighed well over two hundred pounds. Milo had a suggestion of a paunch, but Stuart knew the paunch was just as hard as the rest of him.

There was gray in Milo's black hair, and it was thinning over his forehead. Milo's eyes were hard and shrewd and gleaming with the same excitement Ivy had shown.

Ernie was grinning. His teeth were white and strong in his young, meaty, brutal face.

Ivy finished rubbing down his lathered horse and turned to catch another. Milo Post said heavily, "Uh-uh. You stay here and keep an eye on things. We might be gone a couple of days."

He untied the reins of the horse that wore his saddle and led out toward the house, a two-story, squared-log building surrounded by bare ground and odds and ends of equipment and machinery. Bedrolls and gunny sacks of food were stacked on the ground beside the back door. Each of the three men tied a blanket roll and sack of grub behind his saddle. Each shoved a Winchester into his saddle boot.

The old man swung up and said, "Let's go."

He rode out of the yard, up the lane through the hayfield, and crossed the road. He began to climb his horse through the sagebrush and cedars that dotted the benches below the rim. Stuart looked back from the crest of the first low hill and saw Ken Ivy standing in the yard watching them.

Orange from the sun-dyed clouds stained the land. It faded before they hit the trail, and they climbed across the talus slide in the first gray light of dusk.

Unspeaking they rode, stopping occasionally to let their horses blow. The old man kept the lead. Ernie followed. Stuart, the youngest, brought up the rear.

That vague dread stayed with him. If the rustler turned out to be Hugh Shore . . . With any of the others, Milo Post might be content to recover the cattle and turn the thief over to Dan Mountain, the sheriff at Sapovanero. With Hugh Shore it would be different. Ten years ago Hugh Shore had married the woman Milo Post was courting. She'd sickened and died a couple of years later, and Milo still swore she had died because of Hugh Shore's neglect. Nor was that all. Nora Dykes had promised to marry Hugh a month ago, and had told Milo she didn't want to see him again.

No. If it was Hugh Shore driving those stolen cattle down Salt Wash, he'd never see the sheriff or the jail in Sapovanero.

The trail switched back and forth across the shaly slide, ever climbing toward the towering, hundred-foot-high rims above. Where it reached their foot, it was cut out of the solid rock of the rim and narrowed to a foot and a half or less. Above the rim, it disappeared into the spruces before coming out onto the top of the rolling, grassy plateau.

Stuart Post watched his father and older brother with quiet, worried eyes. In some respects, they were very much alike. Both appeared hard and competent, and they were that, if nothing else. But there, the resemblance ended. Ernie, at thirty, was savage and vicious all the way through. Ernie thought gentleness was weakness. He had patterned himself after Milo, but he'd never seen, as Stuart had, the core of decency and sentiment that lay beneath old Milo's tough exterior.

Stuart hadn't seen it often. Half a dozen times in the course of his life. The night his mother died, when he was seven. Once, when he'd wandered into the house and found Diana McGraw, who later married Hugh Shore, in his father's arms. Again, at fourteen, when he'd had pneumonia and nearly died.

But those few times had been enough—enough to understand the conflicting forces that warred within his father's mind. Enough so that he patterned himself upon the good in his father's heart, instead of the harshness which was all Milo ever showed to the outside world.

Their horses reached the foot of the rim, and scrambled upward over the rocky, uneven trail. In a place or two, Ernie and Stuart held back and let their father go ahead, in order to avoid falling rocks kicked loose by Milo's horse. One at a time, then, they went on.

They entered the brooding, fragrant spruces at first full dark, rode silently through them and emerged upon the lushly rich top of the giant plateau.

This, considering the desperate need of the smaller ranchers down in the valley, was the rankest kind of waste. Every year, more than half this belly-deep grass was covered with winter snow and wasted on the ground. But with Skull guarding the trails, with Skull holding all this by force and threat of force, they could do nothing except grumble sullenly and sometimes, when emboldened by liquor and the opportunity presented itself, to drive off a bunch of Skull's fat steers.

Milo Post rode with assurance across the plateau top. He knew every trail, every ridge and gulch as well as he knew the palm of his hand. Behind him rode Ernie and Stuart, both silent, each thinking his own secret thoughts.

The moon came up in the east, yellow and soft, casting long shadows from the sagebrush, from the men who rode through its spicy fragrance.

The hours passed. At about one in the morning they reached the cut fence, and here Milo dismounted.

"Just as well bed down, boys. Can't trail in the dark."

Stuart dismounted, unsaddled, and picketed his horse to graze. He unrolled his blankets, wrapped himself in them, and lay on the ground. Down toward Salt Wash, a coyote howled, and the howl was taken up by others off toward the rim on the east. Stuart stared at the stars, but he didn't sleep.

Milo began to snore, and after a moment, Ernie joined in strong. Anger touched Stuart. Damn them! What they were planning to do tomorrow didn't bother them in the least.

It bothered Stuart. He knew how Milo hated Hugh

Shore. He knew that whatever Milo did to Hugh would be more revenge for things that had gone before than retaliation for the theft of half a dozen steers.

What, Stuart wondered, did Milo intend to do? Would he turn Ernie loose on Hugh? Ernie would like that. Ernie liked nothing better than to hammer another man insensible with his bony, enormous fists.

Would Milo shoot Hugh? Stuart guessed that pretty much depended on what Hugh himself did when he realized he'd been caught.

He cursed softly under his breath, closed his eyes, and at last went to sleep.

Dawn was only the faintest of gray lines in the east when he wakened. Milo was up, hawking and coughing, running his hands through his rumpled hair.

Stuart rolled his blankets. He tied them behind his saddle, then began to build a fire. When it was blazing good, he poured water from his canteen into the smoke-blackened coffee pot, threw in a handful of coffee and put it on to boil.

Milo went to the break in the fence and began to scout around. He came back shortly and said, "Six steers. One man drivin' 'em. Man's boots are run over at the heels. Hole in one of the soles. Ernie, lead the horses through and then splice that wire while Stuart's gettin' breakfast."

Ernie began to saddle the horses. He led them through the fence, tied them, got tools from his saddle and began to splice the wire. The coffee boiled, so Stuart set it aside and began to fry bacon in the fry pan.

Milo squatted across the fire, spreading his rough,

11

work-gnarled hands to its warmth. Stuart looked steadily at him and asked, "What're you going to do when you catch him?"

Milo met his eyes, then looked down at the fire. "How the hell do I know? I don't even know we're goin' to catch him. He's got a good sixteen hour start."

But Stuart had his answer, however obliquely it had been given. Milo hadn't said, "I'll take him in to the sheriff." His failure to say it told Stuart what he had wanted to know.

And now he had a decision to make. Before they caught Hugh Shore, he had to know what he was going to do himself. He couldn't be a part of what they were planning for Hugh, knowing the hate that drove his father, knowing the animal savagery that made Ernie eager to do his bidding. Neither could he stay out of it. Cutting away and turning back, refusing either to help or hinder would be both cowardly and alien to Stuart's nature.

He shrugged faintly, poured himself a tin cup of coffee and fished a piece of bacon out of the pan with his fingers.

He put it between the halves of a cold biscuit, and ate it silently, his mind in a turmoil of indecision. Then, resolutely, he put the matter from his thoughts. He could hardly set up a course of action until he saw his father and Ernie preparing to act. But he knew one thing for sure. There would be no hanging. Not while Stuart was alive.

They finished eating, killed the fire, crawled through the fence, mounted and went on at a hard, fast lope.

The trail was easy to follow. The miles and the hours melted away beneath their horses' feet.

They came to the rim on the Salt Wash side and followed the tracks down through the rimrock trail. Far in the distance, more than ten miles away, Stuart saw a cloud of dust.

If the others saw it, they gave no sign. But Stuart knew them. They must have seen.

Obscure resentment touched him. Damn it, Shore could have been less stupid about this. He could have taken a few palm and gotten away with half a dozen steers without leaving a trace. It was almost as though, in defiance, he had deliberately left this trail.

With a small part of his mind, Stuart could understand and even sympathize with Shore's defiance. This year had been worse than most. There'd been no rain since early in May. Colorow Creek was completely dry at Skull's lower boundary. If it hadn't been for the trickle that raised in its bed a mile farther down, the ranchers in the lower valley wouldn't even have water to drink.

They'd watched their hayfields burn under the blistering sun. The only water being that trickle in the creek, their cattle had refused to go high enough in the benches to get enough to eat. Instead they stood all day down beside the creek, bawling because they were hungry. Desperation made men do funny things. It made them defiant and reckless of consequences.

Nor was there any use pleading with Milo to turn part of Colorow Creek back into its bed. There was no use begging him to lease a part of the plateau top to those who needed it so desperately.

Stuart had tried that, early in the spring. All he'd gotten for his pains was a contemptuous lecture on looking out for himself because, by God, nobody else would. And when he persisted, Milo angrily reminded him of his age and said that if he didn't like the way Skull was being run, he could pack up and leave.

Now he wished he had, because in a couple or three more hours a showdown over the fate of Hugh Shore was coming up. And that was a showdown that Stuart couldn't win.

He could try, though. He could do that much.

The land dropped sharply now. They slid down the trail into the blistering dry heat of Salt Wash, where the ground was covered with alkali that sometimes looked like snow, where nothing grew but an occasional, dried-up greasewood bush.

Dust raised in a cloud from the hoofs of their horses. It settled on their clothes, clung to the sweat on their faces, choked their nostrils and their lungs.

In early afternoon the heat was terrific. For ahead, in the yellow haze that lay in the air, the river shone, twisting like a snake westward toward the Utah desert. Trees on its banks stood out prettily like a beckoning mirage. They were gaining on the rustler at the rate of about three miles an hour. Stuart hoped the rustler would see their dust, drop the cattle and make tracks out of there. Somehow, he didn't think he would.

Milo began to crowd his horse, whose sorrel hide gleamed with sweat. The sour stench of the horses was

14

so thick in the still, hot air, you could almost cut it with a knife.

And then, at a little over a mile, Stuart clearly saw the rustler, saw him turn and stare back upcountry toward his three pursuers. And he recognized Hugh Shore.

With the Skull men so close, Shore's better judgment finally got the best of his reckless defiance. Leaving the cattle, he spurred away downcountry.

A useless, belated thing. Shore's horse was twice as tired as those of Milo and Ernie and Stuart Post.

Milo spurred into a hard, fast run. Ernie kept close at his heels. Stuart stayed about ten yards behind.

As they passed the cattle Shore had dropped, Milo turned his head and roared, "Take 'em home, Stu! We can handle this."

Stuart hesitated only the briefest instant. Then he shook his head and rode on.

Milo had offered him an easy way out. A way to avoid a showdown and perhaps to ease his conscience later. But an out he couldn't take.

Down the steeply sloping, barren valley they thundered. A mile from the river, Shore hipped around in his saddle, gun in hand, and began to fire at them.

None of them paid Shore's shooting any mind. The man was firing from a horse leaping and dodging greasewood clumps, washouts and outcroppings of yellow shale. The chances were greater that his three pursuers would be hurt by a fall than that they would be hit by one of his bullets.

Then his gun was empty, and while he tried to reload,

15

Milo spurred ahead recklessly, took down his rope, dropped the loop neatly over Shore's head and shoulders, and dragged his heaving, lathered horse to a halt.

Shore left the saddle, thumped on the ground, rolled and slid a few feet into a thorny, stunted, greasewood bush and then lay still.

Milo dismounted. Coiling the rope as he walked, he went toward the still, twisted form of Hugh Shore lying on the ground.

Stuart pulled his horse to a halt and sat his saddle tensely. Ernie grinned with cruel anticipation that made Stuart feel a little sick. Nerves were jumping in his body and dread was a coldness in his spine.

The trouble was about to begin.

CHAPTER TWO

Milo Post toed the still form of Hugh Shore, turning him over on his back. He swung his shaggy buffalo head toward Ernie, saying, "Bring me that canteen."

Ernie dismounted, unhooked the canteen strap from the saddle horn and carried it to his father. Milo unscrewed the top and poured a steady stream of water onto Shore's upturned face.

For a while there was no reaction. Then Shore opened his mouth, gasped, and rolled onto his side, choking.

Milo watched him impassively. Ernie began to grin, and Stuart hated him for it.

Shore sat up, comprehension dawning in his eyes.

"Get up and get on your horse," Milo said.

Shore struggled to his feet. His revolver was gone, lost somewhere in the brush, but he flicked a glance at the rifle stock that protruded from the boot on his saddle.

Stuart went and got the horse. He led it toward Shore, a recklessness of his own making him ignore the rifle. As Stuart went past, Ernie snatched it from the boot and flung it into the brush, his grin widening at Shore's protest.

"You won't need it," Ernie prowled.

Hugh Shore was a short, wiry man in his late forties. He possessed a pair of steady brown eyes and a face deeply seamed with lines that weather and adversity had put there through the years. His mouth was wide, thin, and bitter. His voice was strong as he said:

"What the hell do you mean by that?"

"Never mind. Get up and ride."

Shore mounted, wincing with pain in his twisted left leg. He settled into the saddle and Milo said, "Head for the river. Don't try to run or I'll dump you again."

Shore turned his horse and rode slowly toward the river. Ernie and Milo mounted and rode along behind him. Stuart brought up the rear.

The orderly way in which both Ernie and his father had behaved so far didn't deceive him any more than it had Hugh Shore. For an instant he considered drawing his gun, forcing his father and brother to release the man.

Then, almost imperceptibly, he shook his head. If he drew his gun he'd have to use it and he knew he couldn't do that. Ernie and Milo would know it too.

17

They'd just take the gun away from him and go on with whatever they planned to do. Stuart hoped they had no more in mind than a beating for Shore, but he couldn't be sure.

They rode along silently until they reached the river bank. Ernie cocked his eyes at a nearby cottonwood and said, "This is all right. Get off your horse, Hugh."

Stuart rode up beside him, seeing Shore's steady eyes waver and pinch down as he looked at Ernie. He glanced at his brother and understood why. All the way down here Ernie had been working. He had a hangman's noose already fashioned in the end of his rope.

Shore yelled, "No, by God!" whirled his horse and spurred him savagely. Milo dropped a loop expertly over his horse's head and dallied the rope to the horn. The horse hit the end of it, whirled and began to buck. Shore pitched sideways out of the saddle.

Suddenly Stuart was free of indecision. He kicked his horse in the sides and rode over beside Hugh Shore, who was struggling to his feet. Anger smoldered in Shore's eyes, but there was also a kind of hopelessness that made Stuart a little sick.

He swung down beside Hugh and said in a swift, low voice, "Take my horse and get the hell out of here while Milo's coiling his rope."

He stepped out from behind the horse, his gun in his hand. He thumbed back the hammer with a click. "Nothing doing," he said harshly. "I don't want to shoot, but there's not going to be any hanging."

He got the break he had hoped for, the moment when

18

both his father and Ernie sat frozen in surprise.

Beside Stuart, Hugh Shore had lost no time. Swinging to Stuart's horse, he sank his spurs in deep. The horse half reared, then whirled and plunged away.

Stuart's breath sighed softly out. Mounted on Stuart's horse, with a fifty yard lead, Shore would have a chance. Not much of a chance, but a chance. When they got back to town, Milo could swear out a warrant for him if he wanted to.

But Milo dropped the rope he was coiling and his hand went swiftly to his gun. He yanked it clear. Stuart swung his own gun muzzle toward him, but Milo wasn't even looking at him.

Stuart hesitated, and in that instant Milo's gun blasted. Stuart's horse, bearing Hugh Shore, seemed to stumble. He went to his knees. And for a third time today, Hugh Shore hit the ground.

Milo swung his gun back to Stuart. His voice was a whip: "Put that gun away or shoot it. Make up your goddam mind!"

Stuart holstered the gun. It wasn't in him to kill his own father, no matter what he did. He couldn't even kill Ernie.

Milo said, "Take it away from him Ernie," and watched Stuart closely, an unpleasant, unfathomable expression in his hard old eyes.

Ernie flung his rope, in the end of which he had fashioned the hangman's noose, onto the ground. Swinging heavily from his horse, he approached Stuart. "Gimme the gun, Stu."

Stuart remembered many a savage beating received

at his brother's hands. He saw that cruel, familiar grin and said tightly, "I'll give it to you right in the middle of your ugly face!"

He dropped his hand to the gun. Ernie came on implacably, without a visible trace of fear or uncertainty.

Watching Ernie so closely, Stuart forgot Shore, forgot his father. He was wondering how he could possibly be related to Ernie. He was thinking that brothers could not be so wholly different.

When Ernie was ten feet away, Stuart yanked out the gun. He'd never used a weapon on Ernie before, but he'd use one now. He'd use his gun as he would a club.

Ernie came on, feinted at the last minute, then leaped aside. Stuart swung the gun, palmed in his hand.

Ernie's feint threw him off, as did Ernie's quickly upflung arm. But the gun connected solidly with the side of Ernie's head in spite of it. And the sound of it striking was like that of a cleaver striking bone on a butcher's block.

Ernie staggered aside and sat down hard. Stuart took a step toward him, thoroughly enraged. And then he stopped. Blood from a two-inch gash in Ernie's scalp was running down over his ear and dripping off the lobe. Ernie's mouth was slack, his eyes dull.

Warily, Stuart glanced at Milo, who still held his own gun negligently in his hand. He tried to fathom his father's expression and failed. There seemed to be some approval there, but it faded as Stuart hesitated, within striking distance of Ernie on the ground.

Ernie's eyes began to clear. He shook his great head

and the movement scattered little droplets of blood in the air.

Frustration touched Stuart, and anger too. It almost seemed as though Milo wanted him to kill Ernie, or beat him insensible with the gun.

But why? Stuart had faced Ernie, and fought him, half a hundred times in his life. He'd never backed away or knuckled under. But because he couldn't do Ernie the way Ernie would have done him . . . because Ernie's streak of ruthless brutality wasn't present in him . . ."

Ernie came up with a powerful, unexpected surge. He lunged at Stuart and Stuart dodged, but not quite fast enough.

Ernie's rising body bowled him back, staggering, fighting for balance, knocking the gun from his hand. And Ernie followed, a wicked gleam in his narrowed, smallish eyes.

Stuart recovered his balance and backed warily from Ernie's implacable advance. He knew Ernie's bony fists from past experience, knew how hard they could strike. In Ernie's face he could read his brother's twisted love for inflicting pain.

Anger mounted in him, anger at the brutal quality in Ernie that made him thus. Anger because, fighting Ernie, he was always at a disadvantage. Anger because he liked Hugh Shore and knew what was going to happen to him.

He was sure. Or almost sure. Had he been completely certain perhaps he could have used that gun— used it to cripple Ernie and the old man too if that were necessary. But while there was any doubt at all . . ."

Ernie was chuckling, a low, savage, taunting sound. Ernie enjoyed stalking Stuart. He did it every time they fought. And Stuart knew exactly why. Ernie wanted him to break and run. Ernie wanted him to beg.

He never had and he wouldn't now. And as always, when Ernie failed to make him break, his rage burst all bonds.

Stuart stopped unexpectedly and drove at Ernie. His fist struck Ernie squarely on the nose with a sodden sound. Already flattened, Ernie's nose seemed to burst under its impact. Blood streamed from both his nostrils. He licked his mouth and spat redly, but his eyes didn't flicker or change unless, perhaps, to grow more wicked.

Nor did the blow seem to affect him other than to snap back his head. It neither staggered nor stopped him.

Stuart's hand felt broken. His arm ached from the blow all the way to his shoulder. He'd better stop wasting time pounding Ernie's bony, massive head, or he'd break his hands.

He retreated again, leaping aside nimbly as Ernie charged. Occasionally he slashed at Ernie with his fists. So far, Ernie hadn't struck a blow.

Now, Stuart concentrated on Ernie's belly. Each time he struck he drove a low grunt from Ernie's bloody mouth.

And then, so suddenly that he didn't even see it coming, Ernie's maul-like fist slammed him in the ear.

His head snapped to one side, nearly breaking his

neck. He flew through the air, his feet leaving the ground. He landed limp as a doll and lay stunned, unable to think or even move.

Almost as though he were dreaming this, he felt himself grinning, but he knew the grin was a grimace. Ernie was coming, and would kick him until no consciousness remained.

In a flash of insight, never experienced before, he realized that Ernie hated him, had always hated him. What Ernie hated he wanted to destroy. Yet why Ernie should hate him puzzled him vaguely now, just as the difference between them always had.

Ernie's boot toe slammed into his thigh. He rolled, hugging his belly to protect it, drawing his knees under him. He had to get up!

Ernie's boot struck him again, this time in the ribs. The pain was maddening, but it may have helped clear Stuart's head. He lunged forward and up, staggering but coming to his feet.

Shaking his head, the world reeling before his eyes, he turned to face Ernie.

His brother was coming now, coming for the finish blow. Stuart never quite understood how he managed to avoid it but he did. And as Ernie went past, he sledged him on the side of the neck.

And this one staggered him. Before he could recover, Stuart shambled toward him.

As he moved, he picked up speed, forcing his legs to work faster and faster. He gambled everything on this one last charge, on this one last blow, knowing he'd not strike another today.

Ernie helped unwittingly. He leaned forward and began to come at Stuart. The force of Stuart's blow was increased both by his own forward movement and by that of his brother. It struck Ernie squarely in the throat. Ernie stopped as though he had run into a wall. He gasped for air. His face turned white. He gagged and retched dryly.

Stuart hadn't thought he could, but now he leaped in again, sledging his right and left successively into Ernie's chest immediately under his heart.

Ernie doubled to protect himself, presenting only the top of his head to Stuart's gaze.

Stuart felt a soaring exhilaration. Never before had he come so close to whipping his brother. Exhilaration gave him strength, but it also made him reckless. He leaped in, straightening Ernie with a right uppercut, then sinking his left into Ernie's middle.

Seemingly out of nowhere came Ernie's elbow, cutting him across the face, setting him back on his heels.

Ernie's recovery after that was frightening. Like a snarling animal he followed that blow, landing a brutal right in Stuart's eye, following with a jarring left to Stuart's jaw.

Stuart tried to back-pedal and get away, but Ernie followed, fists windmilling and landing with sickening regularity.

Miraculously Stuart kept his feet in those brief few seconds. But his senses were fading.

He saw the last one coming an instant before it struck. It missed his jaw, and struck him on the side of the neck.

His head flopped sideways. He hit the ground and lay completely still.

And yet he wasn't out. His eyes were open, staring, glassy, but he could see, and he could hear.

He willed his body to move, but not a muscle stirred. Striking his neck that way, Ernie's last blow had paralyzed him. His neck was probably broken and when your neck broke you died. But somehow, he didn't seem to care.

Dimly he heard old Milo's roar, "Enough! He's out! Now let him be!"

Ernie stopped right beside his head, a boot drawn back to kick. Milo said disgustedly, "He had you. He had you down and if he hadn't been so goddam soft, you'd still be lyin' there."

It was an odd sort of state Stuart was in right now, an unreal kind of world. The sounds he heard and the things he saw seemed like things you dream and not the realities you see and hear and feel.

Milo grumbled, "He's more like his ma than he's like me. He'll never harden up. He could have clubbed you with that gun while you were down . . . Oh hell, let's get on with this."

He went out of Stuart's range of vision and Ernie followed him. Stuart suddenly remembered why they were here—remembered Shore—and tried to move again. But he couldn't.

Milo's voice came harshly, apparently speaking to Shore, "You son-of-a-bitch, how many times before this have you helped yourself to my cattle?"

No answer from Shore. But the sharp, flat sound of

25

Ernie's hand striking his face, and Ernie's growl, "Tell him!"

Then Shore's voice, tight with emotion, a desperate kind of defiance that was partly disgust and partly fear: "You'd like to know that, wouldn't you?"

Ernie said, "He'll talk when he gets a rope around his neck."

"Then put it there," Milo said.

There was a brief struggle. Ernie came into Stuart's view again, hauling on a rope. Shore came into sight at the end of it, both hands up trying to loosen it, staggering from Ernie's ruthless yanking on the other end.

Ernie hauled him over under a projecting limb of the cottonwood. He flung the end over the limb, caught it as it came down. He hauled it in brutally. Shore suddenly stopped struggling, and stood beneath the limb, content now to keep his hands between the rope and his neck to prevent it from biting too deep.

Milo's voice said implacably, "How many times, damn you?"

"This is the first," Shore said hoarsely.

Ernie yanked on the rope. He had wrapped it around his thighs and now he leaned back against it. Shore choked, but he didn't pull his hands out from between the rope and his neck. Milo shouted, striding into Stuart's view, "Liar! You stinking liar!"

Shore stood there, helpless but steady, utterly without fear now. Shore had at last faced the reality that he was going to die—that there was no escape.

He said evenly, in a voice changed by the rope's pressure on his neck, "You can kill me Milo, but you're goin' to face something before you do. You're not killing me because of half a dozen steers. You're killing me because you've got to prove you're a better man than me. You're getting even because neither Diana McGraw or Nora Dykes thought so. You—"

He never finished the sentence. Milo lunged at him and slammed him in the mouth with his fist.

Shore's feet left the ground and he swung clear of it for an instant. Then, swinging back, his feet touched it again.

He was sagging against the rope. He was out on his feet and but for the rope's support would have fallen to the ground.

The thought ran through Stuart's mind: Back up a little! Back off, Hugh! You're pushin' him right into it.

But Hugh couldn't hear even if Stuart had been able to speak aloud, and he wouldn't have heeded even if he could. A man with strong pride, he had been mauled and pushed around enough.

Milo stuck his face close to Hugh's. "Damn you, I was goin' to let you off! I got the steers back. But now—"

Shore's eyes burned steadily into Milo's. And then Hugh Shore did the one thing that insured his death. He spat squarely into Milo's face.

Milo backed off, wiping a sleeve across his mouth and nose. He trembled from head to foot for an instant, and then he bawled in a voice that didn't even sound like his own: "Haul him up!"

Shore's feet left the ground with a jerk. Still with his hands inside the noose, he began to make choking sounds. His face turned red, then purple, and finally a shade that was almost blue. He kicked violently with his feet.

Stuart tried to yell, to move, but the only sounds that came from him were a couple of agonized, wordless groans.

He closed his eyes, and even this was an effort. Concentration brought cold sweat to his forehead. He had to move! He had to stop this before it was too late!

But he couldn't move. All he managed to do was roll over onto his side.

When he opened his eyes, he saw that Shore had stopped kicking. Head cocked at an unnatural angle by the noose, he was turning slowly on the rope. He was dead.

Ernie had wound the rope around the tree trunk several times and tied its end.

The slanting rays of the late afternoon sun struck Stuart's eyes, partly blinding him. His neck began to hurt excruciatingly. He moved his head, and realized that feeling was returning to his arms and legs. Not that it would do any good now.

He tried to sit up and as he did so a stream of water from a canteen poured down over his head. He made it up to a sitting position. He saw his father first. Milo seemed pale. He didn't meet Stuart's eyes.

Stuart switched his glance to Ernie, who held the empty canteen. Ernie was sweating profusely and his face had an oily shine. The pupils of his eyes had contracted until they were only pinpoints of black. His mouth was twisted oddly, as though from some strain or perverse pleasure. His hands shook.

Stuart looked at Shore, and a shudder took his body.

Shore's face was reddish purple now, suffused with blood. The veins in his forehead and neck stood out in sharp relief. His eyes were open, bulging, staring. His mouth hung halfway open and saliva drooled from it.

He looked smaller hanging there dead than he had in life. Behind Stuart, Milo spoke. His voice was hoarse and raspy. "Ernie, get on your horse and ride back up Salt Wash. Bring those cattle home."

Ernie took his fascinated gaze from the swinging body, his eyes unnaturally bright. Stuart felt cold. There was something unclean, something not decent about Ernie's intent expression.

Without speaking, Ernie walked to his horse, mounted and rode away.

Milo went over to Hugh's horse, which was tied to a clump of brush. He uncinched Hugh's saddle and flung it to the ground. Then he took the saddle off Stuart's dead horse and put it on Hugh's horse. He said, "Come on, Stu."

Stuart stared at him in amazement. "You're going to leave him here?" His neck was so sore he couldn't move it. His head was exploding.

Anger reddened his father's face, quickly volatile and sharper than necessary under the circumstances. "What do you expect me to do, cut him down and haul him in to Dan Mountain?"

"I don't know what to expect from you, Pa. Unless it's to expect you to act like Ernie does."

"Don't talk to me like that! I'll—"

"You'll what? Shoot me? Hang me? What *will* you

do? How far *will* you go?"

Milo Post glared at him, but in the end he lowered his eyes. He growled, "The son-of-a-bitch pushed me! He spit in my face!"

Stuart shook his head wearily. "Don't you ever think? Have you any idea what the consequences of this are? And now that your damned wild animal has tasted blood—"

"I don't know what the hell you're talking about."

"Yes you do. I'm talking about Ernie."

"You're his brother and you're just alike, except Ernie's a man and you're still a snivelin', wet-nosed kid."

Feeling more sure of this than he had of anything in his life before, Stuart said, "We're not alike and he's not my brother. I'm no kin to a pig like him!"

The flat of Milo's hand struck hard against his cheek. "Damn you, don't ever say that again or—"

Stuart rubbed his cheek where the blow had struck.

"More threats, Pa?"

"Maybe they ain't threats."

Stuart knew he was going too far but he didn't care. "Maybe you're getting an appetite for killin'."

Milo, taunted beyond endurance, fairly screamed at him, "Damn you, shut up! Shut up!"

He turned away, trembling. His great hands clenched and unclenched at his sides.

Stuart, trembling almost as badly, walked across to the cottonwood. He untied the rope and eased its grisly burden to the ground. Then he walked over and swung stiffly, painfully, to the back of Hugh Shore's horse.

30

He waited patiently for his father to mount. His mind was sick and filled with a kind of hopelessness that was new to him.

He knew he ought to load Hugh's body and take it to the sheriff at Sapovanero. He also knew he wouldn't. Unbreakable ties of loyalty bound him to Milo, to Skull, even to Ernie.

He might have been able to betray them if it would have done any good. But nothing he did would help Hugh Shore. Hugh Shore was beyond help.

CHAPTER THREE

They turned, and headed for the river. Across its placid width, Stuart could see the road, a narrow, dusty ribbon winding east toward Sapovanero. From here, the town was less than fifteen miles away.

Milo pulled up abruptly. "Somebody's comin'."

Stuart watched him. Milo whirled his horse. "Let's get the hell out of here. Good thing you cut him down." He put his horse into a lope, heading back toward the mouth of Salt Wash.

Stuart followed. Beneath their horses' hoofs a dust cloud lifted on a hot rising wind. Whoever was coming couldn't fail to see them. Recognition would be difficult at this distance, but there was proof enough at the scene of the hanging to tie Skull in with it.

Hidden by the canyon of Salt Wash, Milo Post halted. "Maybe we'd better stick around and see if they find him."

"What difference does it make? One of our horses is

right there next to him."

"Makes a lot of difference." Milo dismounted and climbed up the alkali slope. Stuart stayed where he was. Renewed anger was beginning to grow in him, slow anger that smoldered like a glowing bed of coals. Hanging Hugh Shore had been so damned useless. Milo could have taken him in to the sheriff. Hugh would have gotten two years in the state pen. That would have put him out of circulation for a while; it would have served as a deterrent to other would-be rustlers.

Milo came sliding down the slope. Mounting, he said, "Let's go. They've seen him."

"Who is it?"

"Can't tell. Two riders."

Milo whirled away and headed up the floor of Salt Wash at a lope. Stuart followed.

They caught Ernie about four miles from the river. Thereafter, all three helped push the half-dozen steers Shore had stolen.

Along the baked, arid valley they went, and up the twisting trail to the rim. At nightfall, they pushed the steers through a gate onto Skull range.

Milo closed the gate and swung back up onto his exhausted bay. "Keep your eyes peeled for horses. I want fresh ones before we ride in to the ranch."

They rode until moonrise, and shortly thereafter came upon a bunch of loose saddle stock drowsing at the edge of a thicket of oakbrush. Each man roped one out and quickly changed saddles. Then they turned their played-out mounts loose.

32

Two hours before dawn, they rode into the home place, unsaddled and shooed their horses into the corral.

The house was dark and all the hands asleep. Stuart went to the pump and washed the blood and alkali dust from his face and neck and hair. Then he stumbled up the stairs to his room and fell across the bed without bothering to remove his clothes.

Dan Mountain, sheriff of Ute County, rode in at sunup, heading a posse of seven men. He stepped out of leather, spoke softly to those with him, then crossed the yard toward the house.

Milo, Stuart, Ernie, Ken Ivy and Olaf Gurtler were in the kitchen. Olaf had on a dirty apron and was frying flapjacks on the enormous cast-iron stove.

Milo looked up as Mountain stepped inside. "Come on in, Dan. Olaf, pour Dan a cup of coffee."

Dan accepted the coffee and sipped it standing. He squinted at Stuart's battered face.

"What happened to you?"

Milo answered quickly. "Him and his goddam brother! They'd rather fight than eat."

The sheriff nodded, glancing at Ernie. He sipped his coffee thoughtfully.

He was a short, very broad man. His legs were bowed from a lifetime in the saddle. His eyes, pale blue, were steady and quiet and accusing.

He was a bit of a dandy in his dress, tooled boots, whipcord trousers and a lightweight wool shirt. He wore his sheriff's badge pinned to the pocket of his shirt.

33

He said, "Hugh Shore was hanged yesterday down at the mouth of Salt Wash."

"Hanged! For Christ's sake, why?"

"There was a dead Skull horse alongside of him."

"You mean he stole one of our horses?"

The sheriff shrugged. "Where were you yesterday afternoon, Milo?"

"Where I always am, this time of year. Ridin', up on top."

The sheriff studied him carefully. "Didn't see nothin', did you?"

"Nothin' unusual."

Dan Mountain looked at Milo steadily, his face faintly flushed. "You're a liar, Milo. You hanged Hugh Shore."

Milo smiled. "Got proof, have you?"

"You know damned well I haven't. Tracks don't last in that Salt Wash country longer'n a June frost. Wind wipes 'em out."

Milo got up. "I like you, Dan. I've always voted for you. But you know better than to come around callin' a man a liar and accusin' him of hangin' somebody, particularly when you've got no proof. Now, I'm willing to forget it if you will. Let's just pretend this never happened."

Dan Mountain said implacably, "I'll get you, Milo, one way or another. I know why you killed Hugh. He took the woman you wanted ten years ago. Worse, he took the one you want now—Nora Dykes."

Fury drained the blood from Milo Post's ruddy face. "Get out of here, Dan. Get out, before I kill you."

Dan Mountain smiled grimly. "Kill me and you

34

won't last five minutes. Every one of those men in the yard was one of Hugh Shore's friends." He turned to go, then swung back.

"Oh. Something you'll want to know. Hugh Shore willed his place to Nora Dykes. She's movin' onto it today."

Milo's voice was tight. "Get out of here, Dan!"

"Sure, I'm going. Just remember what I said." Dan Mountain went out. A minute later, Stuart heard him thunder through the gate at the head of his posse.

Stuart stood up. He strode toward the door. Ernie got there first and blocked it.

"Get out of my way," Stuart said softly.

Ernie looked at Milo. Milo said, "Let him go."

"He might go to the sheriff."

"Uh-uh. Stu wouldn't turn on his own family."

"Don't count on that," Stu said.

Milo shrugged. There was an expression in his eyes that Stuart had seen in them only once or twice before. Understanding, perhaps. Regret, and certainly a touch of shame. Milo said, "If Stu turns us in—well, I guess it'll be because he can't see no other way out of it. Let him go, Ernie."

Ernie glared at Milo. He licked his thick lips and switched his attention to Stuart. He said, "Don't do it, Stu, or I'll beat you to death."

"Get out of the way."

Ernie stepped aside. Stuart's stomach knotted with hatred as he stepped outside.

He headed for the corral, caught a horse, saddled and rode out. He headed downcountry, his mind in a turmoil and tortured with indecision. There was only one right thing for him to do. That was to ride in to Sapovanero and tell Dan Mountain what he knew. Yet how could he betray his own father and brother? If he did that he'd never be able to live with himself afterward.

Only briefly did he consider running away. Then, looking up at the brooding rims, looking down at the valley, already shimmering with rising heat, looking at the spreading fields, he knew he couldn't do it. This was his home and he loved every inch of it. Besides, there was Katie Dykes . . ."

Just thinking of her made him feel better. He began to hurry.

When Dan Mountain brought the news of Hugh Shore's death to Nora Dykes early in the evening of the same day he was hanged, he thought she took it extremely well. Outwardly, at least. Nora took most things well outwardly—the slights and outright rudenesses heaped upon her by the women of the town—the insulting remarks that men passed in her hearing on the street.

She was a tall, full-bodied woman, her beauty only slightly faded by her thirty-five years. There was warmth in her eyes, softness and fullness to her mouth.

Yet for all the impression of softness, Dan had always felt that she had a lot of steel in her too. He suspected that if Nora Dykes ever hated, she would hate exceedingly well.

The town knew what she was—what she did for a

living. Dan Mountain had often been upbraided by one or another of the town women because he failed to run her out.

But she was discreet and careful, and besides that, Dan liked her. Additionally, he knew her continued presence in the town got him more votes from men on the country's outlying ranches than he lost from the influence of women here in town.

He had visited her a number of times himself, and had enjoyed it every time. She knew how to make a man feel virile and important. She made more of the relationship she offered than any of the women Dan had known in the past. Nor was there ever any hurry about it. Nora would sit in her parlor and drink with a man, and talk, and later would take him into bed with her. She had a way of making him feel she was more interested in him as a man than in the money he was paying for her favors.

She sat quite still for several minutes after Dan told her Hugh was dead, and then she asked in a still, small voice, "How did it happen, Dan?"

"He was hanged, Nora, about twelve miles down-river from town."

Her face whitened slightly. "Who did it?"

Dan laughed harshly. "Ain't much doubt about who, though proving it will be something else again. There was a wind all yesterday afternoon and most of last night. It scoured Salt Wash clean of tracks. It was Milo Post, Nora. I'd bet my badge on that."

"Why?"

"I suppose Hugh stole some cattle. I have an idea he

37

was driving them down Salt Wash, intending to sell 'em to the slaughterhouse in River Bend."

Nora's full mouth tightened. Then tears brightened her eyes.

"What is it?" Dan asked.

She looked straight at him. As always, he found her eyes disturbing. She said in the barest whisper, "Then it's my fault."

"How the devil do you figure that?"

"We were getting married. You knew that. Hugh kept talking about wanting to fix up his place for me before-hand. A couple of times he said he wished we could take a honeymoon trip for a week or so. But he didn't have any money, and his own cattle are too thin this year to sell."

She twisted her hands together in her lap.

"Hugh was the only man who ever asked me to marry him, Dan."

Dan reddened slightly. He had nothing to say.

"I know it wasn't fair," Nora said. "Everybody knows what I am, and it would have been hard on Hugh until people forgot—if they ever did. I guess I was selfish, Dan. But Katie—"

For the first time she lost her composure. She turned her face away, and sobs shook her shoulders.

"I wanted to be respectable for her, Dan. I've seen the way she holds her head so high as she goes along the street, as if she were daring them to say anything. I know how hard it's been for her, and I wanted to make it easier. I'd have made Hugh a good wife. I'd have been true to him. And if I couldn't love him, he'd never have known."

38

Dan cleared his throat. "I'm sure of that, Nora." He sat there feeling embarrassed, and then he remembered the scrap of paper in his pocket. He dug it out. "We found this on him, Nora. From the way it's scrawled, I'd say he wrote it while he was riding. Probably while they were chasing him. It says he leaves his place to you."

Now she began to cry in earnest. Dan got up and went to her. He patted her shoulder awkwardly. "Don't you be blamin' yourself now. Hugh knew what he was doin'. He knew what'd happen if Milo caught him."

She mopped her reddened eyes with a scrap of a handkerchief. "Thank you, Dan."

Dan studied her a moment, twisting his dusty, broad-brimmed hat around in his gnarled hands. "What are you going to do?"

She looked up, something hard, something almost unpleasant in her expression. "I'll take the place, Dan. I was intending to go live there anyway. The only difference now is that Hugh won't be there with me."

"Two women can't—"

"Can't run it? I think you know me better than that, Dan."

"Damn it," Dan said irritably, "there wasn't a living on that place for Hugh. How he ever figured to support a wife and daughter is something I'll never understand."

"He told me several times that things were going to change. He said Skull had held the water and the range long enough."

Dan frowned. He wondered what Hugh Shore had known to make him voice such an unlikely prediction.

39

Skull wasn't about to release any water or lease any range. Far from it.

He said, "Then your mind's made up? You won't reconsider?"

"No Dan. Hugh wouldn't have left me his place if he didn't want me to take it. It's the least I can do for him. Besides, I have to live. And with Katie home to stay—"

Dan shrugged. He said goodbye, put on his hat and went out the door. On the walk he stopped to light a cigar and stare speculatively back at Nora's house.

It was a big, two-storied house which she rented from the estate of a man who had formerly lived in Sapovanero. She had lived alone in it all these years while Katie was growing up, cared for by Nora's sister in Denver. A couple of months ago, the sister had died, and Katie had come here.

Awkward for Nora, Dan thought sympathetically. She'd tried to keep Katie from knowing how she lived, but she hadn't succeeded.

She had quit, though, and she'd finally agreed to marry Hugh Shore, knowing that however hard life on his tiny ranch might be, it would at least offer a means of support Katie needn't be ashamed of. Now she was frantically clutching at another chance, still hoping she could keep Katie with her, still hoping to provide a decent home for her.

Well, maybe it would work. Dan certainly hoped so. If a woman wanted to change her way of life as desperately as Nora did, she sure deserved a chance.

He turned away, sighing. People didn't always get

exactly what they deserved. It would be a lot harder than Nora thought it would.

CHAPTER FOUR

You could ride down Colorow Creek for ten miles from the ranch house before you hit the five-wire fence, which was Skull's lower boundary.

Here, the vast difference between what Skull had and what their neighbors had was very evident. On the Skull side of the fence, grass grew. Below it was nothing—just bare ground.

Stuart Post opened the gate without dismounting, rode through and closed it behind him. He lifted his horse to a steady trot.

Down along the creek bed, he could see the red shapes of cattle, poking along the stream bed looking for water. Even at a distance of more than a mile, he could see how thin they were. Farther on, he saw half a dozen buzzards circling, waiting for one of the weaker cows to die.

He wondered how the buzzards knew a thing was going to die. Did impending death have a smell that traveled for miles through the air, or did buzzards depend on sight? Probably sight, he decided, remembering times when the ugly carrion eaters had come drifting in with the wind . . .

He was strongly depressed today, and the sight of his neighbors' range and cattle only served to intensify that mood. He thought of Katie Dykes, and of her mother, moving up to Hugh Shore's place. Nora must

41

be out of her mind to think that she could make a living there. Shore hadn't been able to.

His jaw hardened. If she meant to carry on up at Shore's ranch the way she had in town . . .

Stuart had a great deal of youth's intolerance for Nora's profession. It angered him because it had hurt Katie. She hadn't known until she'd returned to live with her mother a couple of months ago. The shock of finding out had been rough on the girl, but her loyalty in the face of such shame had remained steadfast. Stuart shook his head, wondering at it.

The thing to do, he thought, would be to marry Katie and take her away, even if they hadn't known each other very long—if she'd agree, of course—and let the problems of Nora Dykes, Milo Post and Big Brother Ernie remain their own. Let them solve them if they could. There was no reason why Katie's life should be twisted by what her mother did, no reason why Stuart should be responsible for Milo and Ernie's acts. It scared him to think that if Katie stayed, eventually she would become like her mother, and that he himself would become as brutal and overbearing as his father and Ernie. And yet, leaving seemed like cowardice, like running away.

He began to hurry his horse, and after another fifteen minutes rode into the yard of the first of the lower valley ranches, that of Hugh Shore.

He stared at the house. It was a small, three-room affair built of notched logs and chinked with concrete. Shore had raised it himself more than fifteen years before. The yard had been raked and tidied, probably in anticipation of Nora's arrival as his bride. It seemed strange to sit looking at the marks of the rake in the ground and to realize that the man who had made them was dead.

Behind the house was another small log building that Shore had originally intended as a bunkhouse for a hired man. He'd never had one, and lately had used the building to store feed and supplies. Stuart scowled darkly. Katie would sleep out there, he thought, while Nora was entertaining customers in the house.

Abruptly he whirled his horse and set his spurs. He rode back to the road and headed for town, traveling now at a steady lope.

If he gave thought to the danger of riding along this road, he didn't let it show. But he was aware that it involved some risk. These valley ranchers were bound to be outraged over the hanging of Shore. Already bitter, they might very well try to bushwhack any member of the Post family who traveled it.

Today, however, he should be relatively safe. The sheriff's posse was less than half an hour ahead of him. And the sound of a shot carried for miles here in the valley, always echoing back and forth from rim to rim.

One by one he passed the lower valley ranches. Rifkin's place, below Shore's. Then Nick Stamm's place—and Stuart recalled with vague uneasiness that Wally, Nick's son, was back from his wanderings, packing a tied-down gun, bragging that he'd killed three men.

A mile below Nick's place was that of Vince Doyle and below that by less than a quarter mile, Tim

Boorom's ranch.

After that it was high greasewood all the way to town.

He met the Dykes' high-piled wagon load of household goods less than a mile outside of town, and pulled aside to let it pass. Nora held the reins clenched in her hands. Katie sat beside her, a tall, straight, slim-bodied girl of seventeen, who had a poise and pride about her that always made something catch in Stuart's throat.

He turned and rode beside the wagon, face and neck red with embarrassment. Over the sound of the iron wagon tires on the hard-packed road, he called, "Movin'? Can I help?"

Nora stared at him with plain dislike. Katie glanced at her mother, then back at Stuart. He could sense all the doubt and uncertainty in her. Probably both Nora and Katie thought he had helped hang Hugh Shore. To them, suddenly, he had become an enemy.

He wanted to tell them that he'd fought his own brother to save Hugh's life. But he couldn't. Anything he said in his own defense would condemn both his father and Ernie.

He paced the wagon, watching Katie's face. He saw the flush creep into it. At last she turned and met his steady gaze. "Of course you can help." She smiled, then, as if to say that she knew Stuart and was sure that he could have had no part in Hugh Shore's death.

Stuart grinned back, his mood of depression lifting almost magically. Thereafter he paced the wagon, dropping back occasionally where the road narrowed, riding beside it where its width permitted.

Once he called, "Think you'll like it up here?"

Katie nodded enthusiastically. Then her eyes clouded and Stuart knew the thought, "Anything would be better than the way it was in town," had been running through her mind.

Yes. It would be better for Katie—if Nora intended to change her way of life. If she didn't, it would be a hell of a sight worse, so far as Katie was concerned.

They reached Shore's place in mid-afternoon. Nora drove the wagon up before the door, and Stuart tied his horse at the corral and walked across to the wagon.

He began to remove the canvas covering. Nora and Katie went inside. As he started to unload the wagon onto the ground, clouds of dust rolled out of the front door. The two women were sweeping with a vengeance.

He worked steadily all afternoon, until well after sundown, until dusk crept down from the brooding, towering rims. By that time, the house had been swept and scrubbed, and all of Katie's and Nora's things moved inside.

Stuart led the wagon team to the creek, watered them in its spare trickle, then started back toward the corral. He saw Katie coming from the house and stopped to wait for her in the locusts that lined the bank of the creek.

Ever since her arrival, Stuart had been courting Katie. He'd had supper a couple of times with Katie and Nora at their house in town. He'd taken Katie to two of the dances at the Odd Fellows' Hall. He'd kissed her once.

Now, watching her come toward him across the

45

darkening yard, tired and dusty, her hair mussed, her face smudged with soot from the stove, he felt a tenderness, a yearning, so intense that it surprised him.

Her voice was young and clear and strong. "It was good of you to help us, Stu. Especially after the way Mother treated you. You mustn't blame her, though. She thinks your father killed Mr. Shore."

She stopped three feet away from him. She brushed her dark, silky hair away from her forehead upon which was a faint shine of perspiration. The gesture was one which Stuart found oddly appealing. She looked up at the rims, shrouded with darkness, visible only because the sky above them was lighter than the rims themselves. "It's beautiful here, Stu. I'm going to like it."

Stuart didn't reply.

Katie stepped closer. "We're going to make it work, Stu. Mother's changed. All that—all that other is past."

"I hope so, Katie." His own hoarseness startled him. Then he said, "Katie—I—"

"What is it, Stu?"

"Why just this. You know where I am. If you need help—or anything—you know where I am."

He was remembering the time he had kissed her, remembering too that the kiss had seemed to frighten her. Now he stepped toward her and put his arms around her. He could feel her body stiffen. He could feel her beginning to tremble slightly. He said, "Katie, you're not afraid of *me?*"

She pulled herself free almost frantically. She turned her back to him.

"Katie?"

"I'm not afraid of you Stu. It's—"

Stuart felt a surge of understanding, and of anger too. He knew what was bothering Katie. All physical contacts with men reminded her of her mother's former profession.

He put his hands on her shoulders and his voice was very soft. "I won't rush you Katie. Only don't let your mother spoil your life."

He kissed her lightly on the neck. She jumped, almost as though she had been burned. Up at the cabin, the door opened, framing Nora Dykes with light. Nora called, "Katie!"

"All right, Mother."

Katie walked toward the cabin. Stuart kept pace. At the edge of the light circle cast by the open door she stopped. "Supper will be ready soon. Come in as soon as you've put the horses away." She turned toward him suddenly, stood on tiptoe and kissed him on the cheek. Then, her face flaming, she ran for the house, went in and closed the door.

Stuart put the team in the corral. His own horse was still tied to one of the corral poles. Excitement ran strong in him as he thought of Katie. He could see a lot of her now. It was only eleven miles from Skull to Shore's place. He could ride down often in the evening after his work was done.

But . . . no, it wouldn't be so easy. After all, Milo had been one of Nora's callers before she got engaged to Shore. Milo didn't love Nora, and wouldn't have married her. But he'd been furious the last time he'd gone to Nora's place in town, only to be turned away. Now, with Shore dead, with Nora this close, Stuart wondered if Milo wouldn't try again.

He almost groaned aloud. That would just about cook him for good with Katie.

He shook his head violently, angrily, to clear his thoughts away. He crossed the yard to the house. He knocked lightly and opened the door.

Both Katie and Nora had washed and brushed their hair. Supper was on the stove. There was a strong odor of soap and stove polish in the air, mingling with the satisfying odors of cooking food and coffee.

Katie said, "Sit down, Stu. I'll bring you some coffee."

Stuart pulled out a chair and sat down at the table. It was covered with new oilcloth. Katie brought him a cup of coffee and he sipped it appreciatively.

A kind of drowsy pleasure crept over him. For as long as he could remember he had lived in a woman-less, untidy house that contained only the bare essentials of existence. Olaf Gurtler was a lousy house-keeper and not much better as a cook. Since it was all Stuart knew, he hadn't particularly minded the discomfort. But now . . ."

He heard a horse come into the yard, and tensed in spite of himself. Outside the door a saddle squeaked as somebody swung to the ground. There was a light knock on the door.

Stuart half rose to his feet, but Nora said quickly, "No. I'll go." She was pale and he saw something like fear in her eyes.

48

She opened the door. Looking past her, Stuart saw a man on the stoop, a young man about his own size but perhaps a trifle more slender. The man did not remove his hat, and there was a sly smile on his face. He said, "Nora! Am I the first? Say now, this is going to be handy, bein' neighbors with you."

Stuart had only seen Wally Stamm once since his return, but he recognized him instantly. Nora made a move to go outside, but Stuart beat her to it. Shoving her aside, he went out, pulling the door behind him.

He stood with the door at his back and said, "Go on back home. There's nothing here for you."

In the darkness he couldn't see Stamm's face clearly, but he could hear the incredulous note in Stamm's high voice. "Man, you don't lose much time! Already got it nailed down, huh?"

"Nothing's nailed down. I helped them move in today. But you're in the wrong place. You've made a mistake. There's nothing here for you."

"Well by God! Got the Skull brand on 'em already! Skull's got to have it all, don't it?"

Stuart said softly, "Keep your voice down."

"The hell I will!" Wally shouted. "I got Nora's price an' I'm goin' in!"

The shout could not possibly have failed to carry to the two inside. Stuart could almost visualize Katie's stricken expression, the flush of shame that would be on Nora's face.

Wally tried to push past him and reached for the doorknob.

Stuart swung hard, and his fist smashed Wally

49

squarely between the eyes. Staggering backward, Wally yanked his gun.

He fell, and Stuart lunged at him, wishing frantically that there was more light. He kicked out, hoping to connect with Wally's gun hand, and connected instead with his head.

Wally groaned. Stuart fell on him, groped wildly, and succeeded in seizing the muzzle of Stamm's gun. It blasted as he twisted it away.

Stuart fought to his feet. Panting, he ejected the empty and the remaining live bullets from the gun.

"Get up and get the hell out of here," he said.

Wally got up. Fury emanated from him, almost tangible in the darkness. He said, "I'll kill you for this."

"Real bad, ain't you?"

"And I'll come back. Hell, she's anybody's woman—anybody's that's got her price!" Wally's voice had risen again.

Stuart slapped his face, back and forth, half a dozen times.

"Open your dirty mouth again," he said, "and I'll close it for good."

Wally didn't reply this time. He walked across to his horse and swung to the saddle. Stuart said, "Catch!" and tossed the gun to him.

Illuminated by faint lamplight from the window, it turned over and over in the air. Wally caught it. His voice was a savage whisper. "You're dead, Stu. Your whole damn family's dead. You went too far when you hanged Shore. Now some of the rest of us are goin' to have what we should've had years ago—water—

50

range—all the rest of it!"

Stuart didn't say anything, and after glowering down at him a moment more, Wally Stamm spun his horse and pounded away into the darkness.

The door opened. Both women were terrified. He could tell that, and suddenly he felt much older than his twenty years. He said, "It's all right. He's gone."

"Yes." Nora's voice was lifeless. She turned and looked at Katie. "I'm sorry, Katie. I'm sorry."

Katie fled to her mother's arms, her shoulders shaking with sobs. Stuart softly closed the door and strode to the corral. He chinbed his horse and rode upcountry in the direction of Skull.

Anger that had smoldered in him for the past few days was steadily growing, like a grass fire fanned by a rising wind. And as he rode he carried with him a grim certainty. The days of uneasy peace had gone from the valley of Colorow Creek. There was trouble ahead in the days to come. Violence would rage from one end of the country to the other.

And all because of the hanging of Hugh Shore. All because of a stupid, needless act of vengeance.

Stuart knew he couldn't stop it. All he could do was to stand in the middle, trying to discourage the excesses on both sides. That, or run away—and running was something he would never do.

CHAPTER FIVE

Stuart wakened in the morning to the sound of distant gunfire. He jumped out of bed, dressed hastily, and ran downstairs. The house was deserted.

He raced into the yard and across to the corral, buckling his gunbelt around him. He roped out a horse, saddled, mounted, and galloped away toward the continuing sound of gunfire.

It had come sooner than he had expected. He had supposed that they would at least wait until after Hugh Shore's funeral, which was scheduled for today.

The gunfire continued, a steady emptying of guns, almost like rapid fire on an Army target range. That puzzled Stuart. If Skull's crew and the small ranchers were battling it out, it shouldn't have sounded like that.

As he rode, the sun peeped over the horizon in the east. The miles flowed away under his horse's running hoofs, but still the gunfire seemed far away.

He noticed something, then, that he hadn't noticed before. Water was running in the creek. Someone had closed the headgate upstream at Skull's dam, turning the water back into the creek.

He saw something else that startled him—a single bony steer out in the hayfield, gulping grass in huge greedy mouthfuls.

Comprehension struck him, shocking him, making him rake his horse's belly with the spurs. The bunch downstream had cut the fence. They'd turned their starving cattle loose on Skull.

52

At last he understood the gunfire. His father was retaliating with ruthless brutality. Milo Post was down here killing cattle as fast as he could pull the trigger.

From the sound of it, Ernie was with him, and Ken Ivy, and Olaf Gurtler too.

The shooting stopped before Stuart reached the lower hayfield. Riding recklessly, he met Olaf Gurtler while yet half a mile away. He pulled to a plunging halt.

"What's going on?"

Gurtler was a broad-faced, cheerful Swede. Usually his blue eyes were twinkling, his big mouth smiling. This morning, though, he looked a little sick. He said, "You heard. We was killin' cattle. The old man sent me for a team to drag the carcasses out of the hayfield."

Stuart didn't say anything. Olaf grunted, "I better be goin'," and rode away.

Stuart went on at a walk. He crossed the creek and climbed out of it into the lower hayfield.

Carcasses of dead cattle lay scattered about, reddish blobs against the browning grass hay. A few of them, only wounded, kicked feebly.

Ken Ivy looked sick, as Gurtler had. He was trying to roll a cigarette with fingers that trembled. Ernie had a bright shine to his eyes and he was sweating.

Milo seemed untouched by what had happened. Stuart rode to him and said, "Is this supposed to solve things? Good God, when will you learn? You're poking a hornet's nest. Don't you realize that?"

"They cut my fence. Nobody cuts Skull fence."

"They'll do worse than that, to pay you back for this."

53

"Just let 'em try!"

Stuart reined away. He rode out through the slaughtered cattle. He saw the brands of all the lower valley ranches, including that of Hugh Shore. He rode back to Milo.

"Did you have to kill Nora's cattle too?"

"Why not?" Milo tried to meet his eyes and failed. He mumbled, "I'll try to make it right with Nora."

"Sure. Sure you will. But how?"

"I'll pay her for 'em."

For the first time in his life, contempt for his father overcame Stuart. He shouted, "You think you're fooling me? You know Nora's going to try to make that stinkin' little ranch pay so she can make a decent home for Katie. But you won't let her, will you? She turned you down because of Hugh Shore and you couldn't stand it. So this is how you get even."

Milo's arm swung. The flat of his horny hand struck Stuart on the side of the face. Stuart's head snapped to one side and his ears rang.

He waited until his head cleared.

"Does the truth hurt, Pa? Does it hurt that bad? Take a look at yourself for a change. You didn't have to shoot Nora's cattle. You could have let them go. But you don't want her to make a decent living. You want to sleep with her. Hell, you haven't even got as much decency as Hugh Shore had. You won't even marry her." He turned away in disgust.

Ernie rumbled, "Pa, you don't have to take that kind of talk. If you won't kick the hell out of Stu, by God I will!"

"Try it," Stuart said. "Try it and, brother, or no brother, I'll kill you."

Milo roared, "Shut up, damn it! Both of you!"

Stuart felt limp and weak. He said, "I'll tell you what you'd better do now, if you don't all want to die. You'd better send Ivy up on top. You'd better bring in the crew and you'd better do it today—or by this time tomorrow Skull's going to be nothing but a pile of ashes."

Silence like death hung over the meadow. For all the bright sun, for all the summer warmth, a chill crept through Stuart's body. Ivy said, "You want me to go, boss?"

"Maybe you'd better," Milo said. "Get yourself a fresh horse out of the corral. Get 'em back here by mid-afternoon if you can."

Ivy spurred away. Milo said, "Stu, take this rifle and hide yourself in the brush up on that hillside. Ernie, you go down into the brush along the creek. I'll wait until Olaf gets back with the team. We'll drag 'em out of here and you cover us."

Stuart took the rifle and rode away. He crossed the meadow and climbed the hill. He tied his horse behind a towering clump of sagebrush, high enough to hide the animal, then walked to a place from which he could command the cut fence below.

He wondered if, when the lower valley ranchers came, he could shoot into them. He scowled blackly, furious at the position into which his father had thrust him.

Loyalty was a funny thing. It kept him from taking

sides with the lower valley ranchers. It had kept him tied here at Skull, an unwilling participant in the things Milo and Ernie were doing. What had happened this morning couldn't help but alienate him from Katie and her mother. God knew, it would have been hard enough for them to make a living even if they'd had cattle. Without cattle, they didn't have a chance. Nora would have to go back to her old way of life. She'd have no choice.

Nor was that all. The Sapovanero Bank held mortgages on all the places in the lower valley. Hugh Shore's place was no exception. With the ranchers' cattle gone, or even partly gone, the bank would call their notes.

Maybe that was what Milo wanted. Maybe he had a deal cooked up with the bank to buy those lower valley places.

Somehow or other, Stuart doubted that. Milo hadn't gone at this as though he had a plan. No. He'd rushed into it mainly because he was jealous of Hugh for marrying Nora. He hadn't wanted her for himself—not really. Probably he'd just hated to admit to himself that Hugh Shore could take anything away from him, whether it be a woman or six head of Skull steers.

Only he was wrong. Hugh Shore had taken Diana McGraw away from Milo ten years ago. He'd taken Nora Dykes away from Milo only recently. His attempt to take Milo's steers to pay for his honeymoon had just been more than Milo could stand.

If it hadn't been so tragic, it might have been funny. Milo was acting like a spoiled boy. But the consequences of his unthinking acts were going to be terrible.

Stuart made himself comfortable and rolled a cigarette. He lighted it, and drew the smoke deep into his lungs. He wondered when the bunch down the creek would arrive, and what would happen when they did.

The sun climbed in the sky. It was a beautiful day. The rims stood out starkly against the flawless blue sky overhead. The creek made a soft, murmuring sound as it tumbled along. Absently Stuart counted the carcasses of the cattle down in the hayfield. He counted forty-seven.

Not all the cattle belonging to those downstream. Thank God for that. Probably only fifteen or twenty percent. But enough. Enough to ruin any chance the lower valley ranchers had to hold onto their heavily mortgaged houses. Enough to turn Nora and Katie staunchly against Stuart. Enough to start a range war that wouldn't stop until half the men along Colorow Creek were dead.

An hour passed. Down in the hayfield, Milo paced restlessly back and forth. He kept looking nervously downstream.

Stuart saw Olaf Gurtler coming with the team. Olaf was riding one of the horses, his legs flapping against the horse's gleaming, fat sides. He had a gunnysack over his shoulder and a coffeepot in his hand. Stuart grinned faintly. Trust Olaf to think of food at a time like this.

Olaf slid off the horse and handed the coffeepot to Milo. Milo drank from it. Olaf gave him something out of the gunnysack, and Milo ate it standing. Then Olaf walked up the hill toward Stuart.

Stuart took the two biscuits Olaf gave him, and the piece of cold steak left over from last night. He drank some of the lukewarm coffee from the pot. He thanked Olaf briefly and watched the old cook walk down toward the creek.

Downstream, he saw a cloud of dust upon the road. He made out half a dozen horsemen. They were about a mile away.

He yelled, "Milo!" and pointed downstream.

Milo yelled something to Olaf, then began to walk swiftly across the hayfield toward Stuart. He climbed the hill and squatted down beside Stuart, puffing softly.

Stuart didn't speak. He just stared at the approaching horsemen. Not that he was afraid of a fight. No, that was the easiest part of it. But killing men who had done nothing to deserve it bothered him.

They came on until they were just over a quarter-mile away. Then they reined in. Even at a distance of hour hundred yards, Stuart could recognize them all. He saw Grady Rifkin's huge hulking shape, Nick Stamm's undersized, skinny form. Beside Nick was his son, Wally, the one with whom Stuart had quarreled last night at Nora's place.

Vince Doyle was there, tall and soldierly in his saddle, and beside him was Tim Boorom, squat and thick of body. The sixth man was Tim Boorom's brother Jake.

The six just sat there for several minutes. They seemed to be arguing with each other. Once, Stuart saw

Wally Stamm shake his fist. Then, unexpectedly, they reined around and headed downstream again.

Stuart released a long, slow sigh. Milo yelped triumphantly, "You see? There isn't a teaspoonful of guts in the whole damned outfit!"

"Pa!" Stuart said in amazement. "You don't believe that?"

"What else? They'll never have a better chance than they had just now."

He got up and strode downhill. He beckoned for Olaf. Then he drove the team to the nearest steer. He hooked a chain around the steer's hind feet, picked up the reins and drove the team through the cut fence.

All morning, he and Olaf worked. They finished splicing the cut fence just before the sun reached its zenith in the sky.

He beckoned Stuart and Ernie in, mounted and rode toward the house. Olaf followed with the team.

Ernie was chortling, "I'll bet, by God, they won't try that again."

Stuart sighed. He knew the men downstream hadn't given up. The trouble hadn't even begun.

CHAPTER SIX

This first night at the ranch, Nora Dykes did not sleep well. A strange uneasiness kept her awake.

She tried to rationalize it and decided it was due to Wally Stamm's insulting visit and the scuffle Stuart Post had had with him. It was due to the strangeness of her surroundings—to the shocking suddenness of

Hugh Shore's death and to the way he had died.

She had almost convinced herself when she heard horsemen on the road, and then she knew she had been wrong. No. Her uneasiness had to do with things to come rather than things past.

She got up, went to the window and peered at the road. She saw them go by, raising a cloud of dust. She didn't count them, but she had an impression of several horses and several men.

What were they up to, she wondered. An attack on Skull? Shaking her head, she went back to bed.

Later, she heard them again, this time down near the creek. They were noisier this time, whistling, shouting, slapping reins and quirts against their leather chaps. They were driving cattle.

Puzzled, Nora debated getting dressed and going out. But she gave it up. There was nothing she could do. By the time she could dress and saddle a horse, they'd be out of sight.

Still deeply troubled, she returned to bed.

The remainder of the night passed with maddening slowness. She slept only in snatches, and as dawn began to gray the sky in the east, she heard the horsemen returning.

Again she rose and stared toward the road. She saw them go by and counted six.

She waited until they were out of sight, then got up and built a fire in the stove. She put coffee on to boil, dressed, then went to waken Katie.

Katie seemed subdued, worried. Nora realized that her daughter had slept no better than she had herself.

She made breakfast. Katie went outside and washed at the pump, then came back in the house. They sat down to eat, and were eating when the shooting began upstream.

Nora understood at last. Her neighbors had cut Skull's fence during the night. They had driven their cattle in on Skull. And now Milo Post was having his revenge.

A sickening hopelessness possessed her. Some of her own cattle were certain to be among those killed. There was a mortgage of six hundred dollars on the place and cattle. With part of the cattle gone . . ."

And Hugh wasn't even buried. His funeral was today.

Hatred for Milo Post began to grow in Nora's heart. He had hanged Hugh Shore, putting an end to Nora's dreams of a decent, respectable, protected life.

Not content with that, he was now doing his best to make it impossible for her to live here and earn a decent living for herself and for Katie.

The mortgage on this place, as on all the other neighboring places, was long past due. The bank was only carrying them because it didn't want to foreclose. Now, it would have no choice. Milo Post had seen to that.

Nora said nothing to Katie. She began to dress for the trip to town. She wore a black gown and a black veil.

When she finished dressing, she went out to the corral and caught the team. She harnessed them with some difficulty, and drove them across to the wagon sitting before the door. She had just finished hitching

61

up when she heard again the pound of hoofs along the road. She walked out into the center of the yard and waited.

They rode past at a hard gallop, heading upcountry toward Skull. Their faces were grim, their manner determined. Nora stood in the yard and waited. Her face was pale, her hands trembling. In a few minutes she would hear more shooting. More men would die. And why? Because of Milo Post.

Somehow, some way, she'd have her revenge against him. Out of pure spitefulness he had shattered her dreams. She could see nothing in the future but more of what she'd had the past ten years in town. If she wanted to hold this place, she would have to go back to living as she had before.

She crossed the yard to the tiny, one-room cabin out behind the house. She'd have to clean it up. Katie would have to sleep out here.

She opened the door and peered inside. As soon as she returned from the funeral, she'd get at it. By night, if she worked hard, she could have it ready.

She'd go in after the funeral and talk to the banker. Perhaps if she arranged to make regular monthly payments on the mortgage, he'd hold off. The new life she had promised herself and Katie would have to wait— at least until she paid off that damned mortgage.

Anger kept building in her, anger that made her weak, that made her stomach churn. She'd heard no shots upstream, but as she climbed to the seat of the wagon for the drive to town, she heard voices on the road.

With Katie beside her, she drove up the short lane and into the road. She pulled up to wait for them. She heard Wally Stamm shout, "Goddamn it, we should've done something! We should've—"

"Shut up!" Nick Stamm said harshly. "They were waitin' for us, Milo an' Stuart up on the hill, Olaf and Ernie down in the creek. Besides that, I want to give Dan Mountain a chance at this. We'll get a whole hell of a lot farther if we go at this like we had some sense."

"What if Mountain won't—"

"Then you'll get your chance at Milo."

"An' Stuart!"

"Why Stuart?"

"He's one of 'em, ain't he?"

They pulled up beside Nora's wagon. Wally stared at her insolently, then he put his suggestive glance on Katie.

"What happened?" she asked coldly.

Nick Stamm answered. "We cut Skull fence last night and put some cattle in. Milo shot 'em. There's forty-fifty head of dead cattle layin' up there in his lower hayfield."

"What are you going to do?"

"See Dan Mountain. If he won't do anything, we're going to make Skull so goddamn sorry—"

"Uh-huh," Nora said. The men looked at her with varying degrees of curiosity, then reined away and went on down the road.

Nora clucked to the team and drove along in their wake. Katie sat, silent and scared, beside her. They drove several miles before Katie asked in a shocked voice, "Why did they do it? Why?"

"I don't know," Nora said. Then she turned and met Katie's gaze head-on. "Yes I do. I know. Milo Post was jealous of Hugh."

"Jealous?"

Nora nodded. "Milo didn't want to marry me but he didn't want Hugh to have me either. So when he caught Hugh driving off a bunch of Skull steers it was made to order. He hanged him instead of taking him in to the sheriff the way he would have done with anyone else. Then, because they were angry over Hugh's death, because they were desperate and afraid of losing their homes, those men cut Skull's fence. Milo hit back. Now—"

She was proud of Katie just then, proud of Katie's steady eyes, so filled with fear but filled with compassion too. Katie said softly, "Now?"

"Some of our cattle were bound to be among those killed. With part of their security gone, the bank is sure to demand payment on Hugh's mortgage. I'll have to go on, Katie, like I did before."

"You *have* to go on? Isn't there more to it than that, Mother? We can leave this country. We can work. You don't have to go back to the way things were before. Not unless you want to."

Nora's mouth firmed stubbornly. And she faced a truth she hadn't been willing to face before. She didn't want to leave, no matter what. She owned a piece of land, the first she had ever owned in her life. Nor was that all. She had a debt to pay. She wanted revenge against Milo Post for what he had done to Hugh, for what he had done to her. She wanted that even more than she wanted a decent, respectable life for Katie and herself. Suddenly she knew exactly how she was going to get that revenge.

"I've put up with it for years," she said. "You'll have to put up with it now."

"Mother, please!"

"I'm not going to talk about it, Katie. I'm not going to lose this place of Hugh's. We're going to stay and one way or another we're going to make it pay."

"Maybe you want—" Katie stopped. A painful flush crept into her face. She said, "I'm worried. I didn't mean to say that or even think it."

Nora knew what Katie had been about to say—that maybe Nora wanted her to go into the business too.

She drove along in silence, more bitterly ashamed than she had ever been in her life. But she couldn't change. Even for Katie, she realized she couldn't give up this land of Hugh's, couldn't give up the revenge she planned against Milo Post.

At nine-thirty, she drove the wagon into Sapovanero and went along the street directly to the bank.

Katie moved over to take the reins. Nora said, "Take the wagon down to the livery barn. Get our buggy instead. Then come back here." Katie drove away. Nora went into the bank.

She was used to the stares she got whenever she came downtown. Speculative stares from the men, some bold, some furtive, but all stemming from the same thoughts. Hostile stares from the women, as though she had no right to live, no right to walk the streets in the light of day.

She went through the barred gate and entered the office of Bob Allerdyce, president of the bank. He stood up and smiled at her, though the smile was guarded. He had visited her several times a year or so ago when he was having trouble with his wife. Now that they were getting along again, he wanted to forget those visits. He said, "Sit down, Mrs. Dykes. What can I do for you?"

"Have you heard what happened up the creek?"

He nodded. "Nick Stamm was in. How many cattle did you lose, Mrs. Dykes?"

She shrugged her pretty shoulders. "I don't know. But since Hugh's place is closest to Skull, I suppose we lost more than anyone else."

"Maybe Milo will pay you for them."

"I won't ask him to! What I want to know is what you're going to do—about the mortgage I mean."

"We haven't much choice. Those ranches aren't worth much. The cattle were the only security we had. We've got to protect ourselves, Mrs. Dykes."

"You mean you'll foreclose?"

"We have to—Nora."

"Supposing I were to make regular payments on the mortgage—say fifty dollars a month?"

"Where would you get . . . ?" He floundered to a stop, his face pink with embarrassment.

"I'll get it." Nora said.

Allerdyce frowned. He pulled at his lower lip with his thumb and forefinger. At last he said, "All right, on one condition. You pay me fifty dollars a month, every month starting thirty days from today. The mortgage is already in default. If you miss one payment, I'll have to take it. Is that fair enough?"

"It's fair enough."

She got up and left the office. In the foyer, she met Grady Rifkin, Stamm, Doyle and Boorom. They nodded at her bruskly, then clumped on into Allerdyce's office.

She went out to the street. Dan Mountain stood at the curb, making a cigarette with hands that shook.

Nora said, "What did you tell them, Dan?"

"I told them they had a civil case, Nora. I'm not going to get mixed up in this damn thing. Rifkin and the rest started it by cuttin' fence. Milo Post finished it by killin' cattle. Both sides are wrong. Let 'em fight it out in court."

"That takes money."

"They should've thought of that before they cut Skull fence," he said sourly.

Nora turned away. She saw Katie driving the buggy down the street toward her. Over at the church, the doors were open. A few people straggled in.

Nora climbed into the buggy, and Katie drove toward the church. A boy of fourteen or fifteen tied their buggy horses, and Nora and Katie climbed down and went inside.

Nora took a seat in the last row. Katie sat beside her. The organ played faintly.

The die was cast, Nora thought bitterly. In the fight that was coming, Skull couldn't fail to win. Dan Mountain had washed his hands of the affair, had refused to interfere. If the controversy went to court, Skull would win because Skull had the money with which to fight.

Nor did the small ranchers have a much better chance if the thing came to violence. Skull could muster eleven men just by calling in its crew. The small ranchers had only six and couldn't hire more.

But if internal dissension tore the Post family apart . . . Nora began to smile faintly and it was not a pleasant smile.

Slowly the church filled. At ten the services began. When they ended, Nora filed past the casket with the others.

The undertaker had buttoned a high, starched collar around Hugh Shore's throat, but it wasn't high enough to hide the ugly blue rope burns on his throat. His eyes were closed, but they hadn't been able to compose his contorted features. The mark of violent death was still on him.

Nora shuddered. Katie began to cry softly. Nora pushed her gently and the pair moved on.

The drive to the cemetery was made in almost complete silence. Again, here, the minister intoned his solemn words and at last it was over. Nora and Katie climbed into their buggy and began the long drive home.

Nora's faint smile returned. Katie looked at her and could not repress a shiver.

CHAPTER SEVEN

When they arrived back at the house from the lower fence, Milo and Stuart and Ernie turned their horses over to Olaf and went to the house. Milo put the coffee on to boil and built up the fire. Then he came back outside and hunkered against the wall of the house.

He said, as he packed his pipe, "Looks like that bunch is licked, but there's no use takin' chances. Ernie, when the crew gets back, you take about three of 'em and go down to the fence. Set up a guard—a man below each rim, a man on the benches on either side of the creek. Stop anyone that tries to come through."

Ernie nodded, grinning. Milo turned to Stuart. "I want you to take Ken Ivy and go out on top of the mountain. Keep an eye on that Salt Wash trail. If they try to get in that way, turn 'em back."

Stuart nodded, hating himself for the relief he felt.

"All right, then," Milo said. "Let's get on up to the dam and turn the creek back into our ditch."

They drank the coffee Milo had made and started out. Stuart doubted if the bunch down the creek would start anything until tonight. They were all attending Shore's funeral, for one thing. For another, they'd want to see the sheriff first. If he didn't do anything, and Stuart was sure he wouldn't, then they'd act.

By that time, Milo would be ready for them. If they tried to get through Skull's lower fence . . .

Stuart felt sick. Damn Milo anyway! Why had he started all this?

At three, Ken Ivy rode in with the crew. Stuart packed a bedroll and some grub behind his saddle, loaded up on ammunition, then waited while Ivy caught and saddled a fresh horse. Ready, the pair set out.

Up through the rim they went and out onto the top of the vast plateau. They rode until full dark, camped, and in the morning, rode again. At sunup they reached the head of Salt Wash trail.

Here they camped again, and afterward took turns watching it.

It was a peaceful and lazy existence. Four hours on, four hours off, throughout the day and night. On his off hours, Stuart slept, or hunted, or hauled water from the spring a mile away.

He built a lean-to shelter, after fetching tools from the cow camp seven miles away. The days passed, and they heard no word from the valley. Stuart worried and fretted about Nora and Katie, about his father and the ranch, about the small ranchers below Skull.

At last, two weeks after sending them here, Milo rode in with a replacement for Stuart, and the pair returned to Skull.

Milo was contemptuous. "Hell, they ain't goin' to do anything. They've had two weeks and they ain't made a move."

Stuart studied him speculatively. Milo had changed, but it was hard for Stuart to determine the nature of the change. Milo seemed more sure of himself. He seemed less edgy, less brooding than when Stuart left to come

70

on top. There was an almost youthful vigor about the way he rode and held himself.

Stuart frowned, perplexed. He said, "You could stop the whole thing once and for all—by giving them a little water—by leasing them part of this range here on top."

Milo hipped around in the saddle and stared at him without answering, as though his suggestion were too ridiculous for consideration.

They arrived at Skull in late afternoon. Milo put his horse away, then grabbed a towel and bar of soap and a change of clothes and went down to the creek to bathe. Stuart observed this with surprise, for Milo never took a bath except on Saturday night and not always then.

Stuart sat down on a bench in the shade of the bunkhouse and rolled a smoke. Every now and then members of the crew would go in or out, nodding to Stuart as they passed. He thought they were growing sullen. Bored, he supposed, with sitting down there at the fence day after day guarding against an attack that never came.

Ernie rode in, whistling soundlessly to himself. He grinned at Stuart as he passed on the way to the corral, an unusual thing for Ernie and one which baffled Stuart even more than Milo's behavior. He supposed Ernie enjoyed this waiting—because he knew at the end of it he would get the chance he wanted to strike again at the lower valley bunch.

Stuart ate with the men and afterward rode out with the relief crew heading for the fence.

Ed Levitt, riding beside him, asked, "Things quiet on top, Stu?"

Stuart nodded. He was thinking about Katie, and gave only a part of his attention to Ed.

"Quiet down here too. Either Milo buffaloed that bunch downstream, or they're just waitin' until we slack off a little."

Stuart grunted assent.

"Not much work gettin' done. Guess both Milo an' Ernie got their minds on what's liable to happen or somethin', though neither one of 'em seems to be losin' any sleep over it. Been goin' off to town nights—like by God there wasn't a damn thing to stew about. But they sure expect us to worry. Eight hours on an' eight off. It's like the Army, damned if it ain't."

Stuart nodded.

"What do you think, Stu? You think that bunch down there is scared?"

Stuart yanked his attention back from the place it had strayed.

"They're not scared. At least they're not too scared. You keep awake down on the fence, Ed. They'll hit you when you least expect it."

It wasn't like either Milo or Ernie to go off to town when there was danger of an attack. But maybe only one of them went at a time.

They reached the fence and relieved the guard. After a few minutes, during which he satisfied himself that all was quiet, Stuart left Ed Levitt in charge and rode toward Nora's house.

He knew things could not forever continue as they

were. Sooner or later one side or the other would make its move. The small ranchers would break through and attack Skull. Or Milo, wearied of waiting, would move against them and force their hands.

There was a light in Katie's small cabin behind the house. Stuart knocked lightly on the door.

He heard steps behind the door and Katie's frightened voice: "Who is it?"

"Stuart."

The door opened. Stuart took a step, and suddenly found Katie in his arms. She was sobbing almost hysterically.

He held her for a moment, then went in and closed the door behind him. Anger at Nora smoldered in him, helpless anger because he knew the cause of Katie's tears and could do nothing at all about it.

"Stu, take me away! Now! Please take me away!"

"Tell me about it, Katie."

She controlled herself with a visible effort. She dried her eyes. For an instant they were downcast, then they lifted and met his steadily. "It's mother," she said wearily. "She's so determined and so full of hate. I tried to get her to leave here, but she won't do it. I—"

Stuart gripped Katie's arms. Looking down at her, he realized how much this proud, straight girl meant to him. More than Skull, more than his father and brother—more than anything else in the world.

Katie didn't have to tell him what Nora was doing. She had gone back to her old way of life. Because of Milo. Because it was the only way she could hold this place.

"And your father," Katie murmured. "And Ernie. I thought she hated them, but I guess she doesn't hate them too much to—"

"Where's your mother now?" he asked hurriedly.

"She went to town. She ought to be back any minute."

"And she left you here alone?"

Katie nodded. He could see that she was afraid, that she was trying desperately to conceal her fear.

"I'll stay here until she gets home," he said.

"No. Don't do that. She might make a scene. She might think—"

Stuart smiled.

"It isn't funny, Stu. She's changed. She's changed so much since the funeral you'd hardly know her. She's hard, and she never used to be that way. It's as though holding on here was more important to her than anything else in the world. It's as though anything she has to do is worthwhile so long as it helps her do that."

"I'm going to stay," Stuart said. "No telling who—"

Katie reached up and gently touched his cheek. "I'll be all right. Please, Stu. Don't be here when Mother gets home."

Stuart nodded doubtfully. "All right Katie." He went out and mounted his horse. Katie watched him from the doorway, looking frightened and lost.

He raised a hand in farewell and rode away. He couldn't really blame Nora for using Milo to undo the damage Milo himself had done. She was fighting now with the only weapon available to her—herself.

He turned toward Skull and touched spurs to his

74

horse's sides. The horse leaped ahead. For a minute or so he rode steadily. Then he pulled to a halt, wondering what had stopped him.

The silence of the night was almost tangible. No breeze stirred. No sound broke the almost complete quiet. And then, so suddenly that it raised the short hairs on the back of his neck, he heard a scream, a woman's scream.

He whirled the horse and raked his sides with the spurs. The startled animal leaped, and broke into a hard run.

He thundered into the yard and flung himself from his horse, running. The main house was still dark. The lamp still burned in Katie's cabin, but the door was closed.

Even before he reached the door, Stuart knew what had happened. Someone had come to see Nora, and finding her gone, had tried to force himself on Katie.

Damn Nora for being weak enough and stupid enough to put Katie into this kind of position! Damn Milo for leaving Nora no more palatable alternative!

The door was locked. Stuart could hear sounds of a struggle inside, but no voices, no screams, only an occasional grunt of exertion.

He stood back from the door and kicked savagely at the lock. The door creaked but did not give. Stuart kicked again. This time the door burst inward, and Stuart followed it.

The man was Wally Stamm. Katie's dress was torn, her hair disarranged, her mouth smeared with blood.

Wally's eyes were terrible. Blood ran down the side

of his face where Katie had scratched him. He flung the girl from him and whirled, his arms tense and slightly bent at his sides. Then he saw Stuart.

"Well, by God! Look who's here!"

Stuart didn't speak. He couldn't.

"I didn't see no claim notices on the door," Wally Stamm said. "Hell, she's no better than her ma. And our money's just as good as Skull's."

Stuart got set to launch himself at Stamm, then stopped. Smashing that foul mouth wouldn't staisfy him now. Not after the things Stamm had said.

"You've got a gun," he said. "You're supposed to be pretty good with it. Let's see how good you really are."

Wally, who had relaxed somewhat, tensed again. Katie screamed, "No! Stop it!" and flung herself at Wally just as his hand streaked toward his gun.

Stuart had never fancied himself a gunslinger nor tried to be one. He'd practiced a lot, as all kids do, and then he'd given it up. But now he surprised himself.

His gun was in his hand before Wally's cleared the holster.

Even so, he couldn't shoot. Not with Katie in the line of fire.

He flung the gun straight at Wally's head. Wally's gun blasted and the bullet tore along Stuart's ribs, burning like a branding iron.

Stuart's weapon struck Wally's forehead and Stuart, immediately behind it, struck Wally's chest with the point of his shoulder. Wally went back, falling, his gun roaring again close beside Stuart's ear.

Falling with him, Stuart put all of his weight and

strength behind the fall. They struck, and breath went out of Wally with a great, gusty grunt.

Stuart grappled for his gun-hand, got it and twisted so savagely that Wally screamed with pain. Then Stuart seized his long hair in both hands and banged his head against the floor, again and again and again.

He became vaguely conscious of someone screaming at him, pulling at him. But not until Katie tangled her hands in his hair and pulled did he under- stand her words.

"Stu! Stop it!"

He pulled away from Wally and struggled to his feet. "All right, Katie. It's your house."

He turned back to Wally and kicked him in the ribs. "Get up! Get out of here. If I ever hear of you coming back, I'll kill you!"

Wally struggled to his feet, panting, his chest heaving. His whole body shook violently, and pure murder showed in his slitted eyes. His voice came out jerkily. "You're fast with a gun all right. You surprised me. But it won't help. You'd better grow eyes in the back of your head, Post. Because you're going to need them. Sure as hell you're going to need them."

"You want more?" Stuart asked. "If you don't, you'd better move."

Wally slunk past him and out the door. He mounted his horse. He called back, "Don't ride alone, you bas- tard. Next time I see you, I'm going to blow you apart!"

He rode away. Up on the road, Stuart heard the wheels of Nora's buggy on hard-packed surface. They turned in the lane.

He looked back at Katie. "I'll be down here tomorrow early. Be ready to leave. You and I are going to be married and get out of this country."

She didn't reply. Her eyes answered for her. Memory of their shining beauty stayed with Stuart all the way back to the house at Skull. He almost forgot the pain of the bullet burn along his ribs.

Almost.

CHAPTER EIGHT

Before going to bed, Stuart made a few minor preparations for his departure with Katie. He had a little over two hundred dollars saved, enough to see them well on their way, enough for them to live on until Stuart found a job. He had no intention of asking Milo for more.

He packed his old, worn carpetbag with his one good suit, some underwear, socks and shirts.

Excitement began to rise in him. But it was dulled by a certainty that he was running out on Milo, perhaps at a time when Milo needed him most. The hell of it was, Katie needed him too. She needed him desperately and he needed her.

Both Milo and Ernie had gone to bed and the house was dark. Olaf Gurtler, of course, was on guard down at the fence along with three others.

He blew out the lamp and crawled into bed. For a while he lay awake, staring into the darkness. His unwilling mind kept seeing the dangling figure of Hugh Shore beneath that cottonwood limb. He remembered the way Ernie had looked, both then and at the time he and Milo had killed the cattle down in the lower meadow.

This was his brother, or so Milo said. But what made them different?

He tried to force his thoughts into other channels, but they kept returning to that perplexing question. What *did* make them different? They'd been raised in the same environment, under exactly the same conditions. A disturbing possibility occurred to Stuart. Maybe I am like him. Maybe it's just never come out.

But he couldn't accept that, for he knew the day would never come when he could stand and look at a man hanging dead from a rope and feel the unclean pleasure which had been so apparent in Ernie that day. It didn't matter why they were different anyway. All that mattered was that they *were*. Ernie's brutishness may have infected Milo, but it would never infect him.

Finally he dropped into an uneasy, tormented sleep. He came out of it with a jerk when he heard his door squeak. His eyes opened, and his sleep-drugged mind sought to comprehend the dark shape standing in the hall just outside his door. He growled, "Who the hell is that?"

"Olaf, Stu. It's only Olaf."

"I thought you were down at the fence. Has something happened?"

Olaf pushed the door wide and came into the darkened room. He wiped a match alight on his pants and raised the lamp chimney. He trimmed it with elaborate care, his seamed, reddish face filled with concern.

Stuart flung back the blanket and sat up. He ran his hands sleepily through his hair.

"What the hell's the matter?"

"Maybe nothing. Maybe plenty."

Stuart fumbled for his shirt. He got sack tobacco and papers out of the pocket and began to roll a smoke. When he had it made, he stuck the end over the lamp chimney and lit it. You couldn't hurry Olaf. When he tried to talk fast, he stuttered. Consequently, he refused to talk until he was ready.

"A while ago," Olaf said, "Ernie rode through the fence. He was headed for Nora's place."

Stuart grimaced with distaste. It made him a little sick at his stomach to think of Ernie and Nora together. He said, "What of it? It isn't the first time. You didn't wake me for that, did you?"

"That's not all, Stu. About half an hour later, Milo came through—headed for Nora's too."

Stuart choked on a lungful of smoke and began to cough. He grabbed for his pants and had them on before he stopped coughing. He said, "Jesus! They'll kill each other!"

"That's what I was thinkin'."

"How long ago was that?"

"Half an hour, I suppose. I came here as soon as Milo went through."

Stuart shrugged into his shirt and pulled on his boots. He grabbed his gunbelt from the bedpost and strapped it on. Then he ran out into the hall and down the stairs.

Olaf followed as soon as he had blown out the lamp. Outside, there was a chill in the air, and a dampness that told Stuart it was well past midnight. The stars were bright and the sky cloudless. A soft wind blew from the west.

Stuart crossed the yard to the corral, running. Tomorrow, thank God, he and Katie would be out of this. Ernie and Milo could destroy each other if that was what they had to do. It needn't ruin Katie's life or his own.

He waited impatiently beside his saddled horse until Olaf mounted. Then he led out downcountry at a hard, steady gallop.

What he and Olaf could do if Milo and Ernie were at each other's throats was problematical. Neither of them would listen to reason. Stuart had tried using force on them the day of Hugh Shore's hanging. It hadn't worked then and it wouldn't now.

An odd premonition of disaster rode with him. Something was happening, or would before the night was out—something that would change Stuart's life, and Katie's. He shook his head impatiently. He was dreaming up trouble and it had to stop. Yet the weight of worry inside his head did not lighten.

The miles between the house and the lower boundary fence seemed to drag, though Stuart and Olaf pushed their horses almost to the limit of their endurance. Stuart kept listening for sounds. Shots. But he heard nothing.

An hour. An hour between Milo's arrival at Nora's place and the time Stuart and Olaf would arrive. A lot could happen in an hour.

They went through the gate at the lower fence galloping, the gate having been opened by the man on guard in response to Olaf's shout. Then they were pounding down the road toward Nora's place.

Stuart cut away from the road, puzzled at the complete silence. There should have been some sound. Shouting. Cursing. Quarreling. Unless either Milo or Ernie was dead.

Then, from a distance of almost a quarter mile, he heard a yell at last. Milo's voice, tight and choked with rage. The words were not distinguishable, but the tone was plain.

With Olaf close behind him, Stuart burst into the little clearing that surrounded Nora's house.

The scene that met his eyes was eerie, unreal, frightening. The door of Nora's house was open, and light streamed from it onto the bare ground of the clearing. Nora herself stood in the doorway, holding a lamp. Her face, even at a distance of fifty feet, was visibly contorted, and her hair in wild disarray. She wore a nightgown and thin wrapper.

Then the figure of Milo Post caught and held Stuart's attention. He stood over a prostrate Ernie, every line of his powerful body expressive of utter, uncontrollable fury. But it was not over. It had scarcely begun.

Stuart guessed that Ernie had been with Nora when Milo arrived. She'd made Milo wait . . . longer than necessary . . . long enough so that when she did appear with Ernie, Milo's temper had reached the breaking point.

A low, rumbling, wordless growl came from Milo's throat. It was born deep inside of him and issued from his lips like the growl of some infuriated giant of an animal.

In the flickering light of Nora's kerosene lamp, Milo's eyes glittered. Shadows hid Ernie's face, but Stuart's imagination supplied its own description. Ernie's expression would be wicked, holding neither remorse nor submission. Ernie would get up in a moment, and when he did . . .

Stuart yanked his plunging horse to a halt and swung to the ground. Katie's cabin, dark and silent, squatted behind the main house. She would be there, in the darkened doorway, or at one of the windows, wakened by that angry bellow of Milo's. She would be terrified.

This was a scene no girl should have to watch. Stuart was grateful for one thing—Katie could not see her mother. She couldn't see the ugly triumph in her mother's twisted face . . . Shock jarred Stuart. Nora had planned this. She had intended it to happen just this way.

He took a step toward Milo.

Ernie came up off the ground like a bull knocked off his feet by a bigger, stronger bull. But unlike a defeated bull, he didn't turn and run. Instead he eyed Milo silently, his only sound that of his breath whistling in and out of his lungs.

Stuart yelled, "Stop it!"

Neither of them heard him. They began to circle each other.

Ernie rushed. Without skill, with only brute power and terrible anger controlling him, he closed with Milo, swung a monstrous fist that struck the side of

Milo's head with a sound like that of a cleaver biting through solid bone.

Milo's head snapped to one side. His knee came up, catching Ernie in the groin. They clinched and toppled to the ground ponderously, like grizzlies locked in mortal combat.

Stuart stared in unbelief. Could this be father and son? Could this be the pair with whom he had lived his life, fighting now like mongrels over a woman like Nora Dykes?

Nausea seized his stomach. No matter who won this fight—if both were left alive—it would be the beginning of a hatred between them that would destroy them both. Nora had won. Nora had achieved her vengeance.

Other men might fight, and stop, and eventually forget both fight and the causes behind it. But not these two. Never Milo and Ernie Post.

Stuart felt Olaf beside him. He heard Olaf's softly breathed, "Jesus!"

But he had eyes only for the two locked in combat on the ground. Ernie tried to gouge Milo with a hooked thumb, but Milo rolled his face into the dirt, hunched his back and heaved Ernie off. He staggered to his feet, in time to face Ernie, who was rising with a splintery, weathergrayed singletree in his hands.

It whistled audibly as Ernie swung it, and would have shattered Milo's skull like an egg. But Milo ducked his shaggy head, and the momentum of the swinging singletree carried Ernie halfway around again. Milo leaped. He sledged Ernie on the side of the neck so hard that Stuart could hear the bones crack. Ernie fell like a stunned steer.

Milo was on him instantly, landing with both knees in Ernie's back. Ernie grunted ponderously.

A combination of such blows, delivered by Milo's bony fist and his knees with all his weight behind them, would have knocked an ordinary man out of his senses. But not Ernie. Instead, the pain of them and their temporary crippling effects only seemed to increase his rage.

A roar drove from his lungs before he lunged to his feet, with Milo clinging there like a cat. Straight as a charging bull, Ernie drove at the cabin wall.

But it was Milo's head that struck, with an impact that shook the house and sounded like the muffled beat of a drum. Milo rolled off Ernie's back, momentarily stunned, and lay on his back ten feet from Nora, gasping like a fish out of water.

Ernie swung a booted foot. It sank into Milo's belly, glanced away. The spur strapped to its heel raked Milo's forearm, drawing blood from the long gash it made.

Milo rolled, doubling and hugging his belly with both arms. Ernie was panting hard from exertion, but he poised himself for another kick. Stuart's hand dropped and touched the grips of his gun.

Ernie was berserk, and after he finished Milo, he might turn on anybody—Nora, or Stuart, or even Olaf. He might even go after Katie, knowing this to be the most effective way of returning Nora's hurt.

But Milo wasn't done. From somewhere deep within

him he drew upon a reservoir of strength, and when Ernie's boot swung, he seized it with both hands.

All Ernie's strength went with that kick, so that when Milo grabbed his foot he lost balance and fell.

Milo clawed toward him. His face, plainly revealed now in the light from Nora's shaking lamp, was white and taut with effort and exhaustion. His eyes were wild. His mouth was twisted, half open. His teeth, turned brown by tobacco, showed through, clenched like those of a snarling wolf.

Both Milo and Ernie resembled animals, two savage animals come from the depths of their caves to fight a battle as old as time itself.

Stuart watched with paralyzed fascination. His hand still touched his gun but he probably couldn't have drawn it had life depended upon his doing so. Only death or complete exhaustion could stop this fight. Stuart himself could only wait.

The triumph had faded from Nora's face. She realized now the full enormity of what she had done. Most amazing to Stuart was that she had gotten away with it. He had thought both Milo and Ernie to be sharp and shrewd. Yet they had taken her bait and swallowed it whole. Each must have believed that Nora loved him. Only that could explain their utter fury now; that and the bitter realization that she had used them, duped them, played them for fools.

Nora was beginning to understand that when the fight was over she, too, had a score to pay.

CHAPTER NINE

On and on and on the battle raged. From the wall of the cabin, the two combatants struggled and rolled and staggered across the clearing and into the brush beyond, where all was dark, where only the sounds of their fighting could be heard.

Back then they came, into the light again. Both were battered, bloody and covered with dirt. Their shirts were literally shredded, and their chests gleamed with sweat in the flickering light from the lamp.

Nora sagged weakly against the door jamb and nearly dropped the lamp. Stuart crossed the yard and took the lamp from her. She sank to the stoop and huddled there, her face hidden in her hands. She wept at last, without control or restraint.

Milo and Ernie fought now with ponderous slowness, though it must have seemed to them that they fought exactly as before. Their blows lacked power, but so did they lack the reserve of strength needed to recover from each blow that landed. They grew weaker, and slower, but the fire died in neither man. Still they hated, with a virulence that was frightening. This might end in stalemate, but the fight was only a beginning. Only death, for one or both, could stop their hate.

Father and son? Suddenly Stuart couldn't believe it. Something was wrong. A father couldn't hate a true son enough to want to kill him. Nor could a son hate a father that much.

Stuart shook his head in confusion. From the side of the house he heard Katie scream, "Stop them! Oh my God, stop them! Please!"

Stuart stared at her mutely. Here, where all was ugly and somehow degrading, she was the one thing of beauty.

He drew his gun and stepped toward the fighting pair. They stood toe to toe, groggily slugging it out. He'd knock them both out if he had to.

But there was no need. From somewhere, Milo called up every last remaining bit of strength. He swung his massive fist with all the weight of his body behind it. It struck Ernie's jaw with a sodden crack.

Ernie swayed. He pitched forward, rolled and at last lay still.

Milo, off balance from the blow, stumbled over his body and fell beyond him. Milo too lay still.

Suddenly the clearing was very quiet. The soft wind still blew from the west. Leaves and brush rustled softly. Up below the rim a coyote barked.

For a long moment Katie stood motionless, watching her mother who wept so softly on the stoop. Then, gathering up the flowing skirt of her wrapper, Katie walked slowly to Nora. She knelt beside her and drew Nora's head against her shoulder. Mutely she patted her mother's shaking back.

"We'll have to borrow your buggy," Stuart said.

Katie didn't reply. Stuart nodded to Olaf and Olaf moved away into the darkness toward the corral.

Stuart set the lamp down on the ground. He took a step toward Katie and Nora, then stopped. There was nothing he could say—nothing he could do. This was something private, between the two of them.

He said, "Tomorrow, Katie. Early. We're still going away."

She glanced up at him, neither confirming nor denying. She helped Nora up and into the house. The door closed.

Stuart cursed softly under his breath. Something had, indeed, changed for Katie and himself tonight. Considering this, he realized that both he and Katie had been daydreaming to think they could shrug off responsibility and go away. Nora and Milo and Ernie had showed them, tonight, how impossible that was.

No. They both must stay, being a part of the ruin that lay ahead, just as they had been a part of all that had gone before.

He heard the jingle of harness rings, and moved away to help Olaf harness the horse in the buggy shafts. Olaf led the horse over to Milo and Ernie. The animal smelled blood and shied. Olaf swore at him.

Between them, they piled Milo and Ernie unceremoniously into the rig. Stuart tied both his own and Olaf's horse behind. He said, "Bring their horses, Olaf. I'll drive the buggy."

"Sure, Stu. Lord what a fight! You reckon they got it all out of their systems?"

Stuart shrugged. He was tired. He was tired of useless hatred, and vengeance that only bred more vengeance. He climbed to the buggy seat and untied the reins. He slapped the horse's back briskly with them and the animal moved away. Olaf came along behind, riding Milo's horse, leading Ernie's.

He urged the horse to a fast trot, and thus went up the road, to be challenged at the fence and passed on through. He did not immediately hear Olaf behind him and guessed the old cook had remained at the fence to relate what had happened to the others on guard.

They'd chuckle slyly among themselves about how thoroughly Nora had gotten even with the Posts. Secretly they'd be pleased, just as everyone else in the country would. Nor would the news of Milo and Ernie fighting among themselves strengthen Skull.

Heretofore the Posts had stood solidly together, three against the rest of the country. Now that was changed. With dissension and conflict at Skull, relations with the lower valley ranchers would become all but impossible. There was Wally Stamm, and there were the others, still furious over Milo's slaughter of their cattle. Now, they would become more bold . . .

Stuart wondered what would happen tomorrow. Surely Ernie wouldn't stay. Milo wouldn't let him stay. And Milo certainly wouldn't leave.

The buggy horse trotted endlessly, and slowly the miles fell away behind. Occasionally Milo or Ernie would groan, or stir, and Stuart would glance uncomfortably at their lumpy bodies. He hoped they wouldn't come to until he reached Skull. He didn't want to watch them have another go at each other. If they tried . . .

To hell with them. If they did that he'd go on without them.

But, except for those occasional groans or stirrings,

they stayed quietly unconscious. At three, he drove into the yard at Skull, with Olaf Gurtler riding along close behind.

Stuart drove the buggy to the front door and got down stiffly. He unhitched the buggy horse and, along with the two saddle horses, led him across to the barn where he watered, stabled and fed the animals. After he finished, he rolled a smoke and blinked blearily at the faint line of gray over the eastern rims.

Almost daybreak. He felt as though he hadn't slept for weeks.

Gurtler came from the corral and together, in silence, they walked across to the buggy. They lifted Milo from the buggy. Stuart took his head, Olaf his feet. They carried him inside and up the stairs where they flopped him down, fully dressed, upon his bed.

Both Stuart and Olaf were sweating heavily and breathing hard. They sat down on the top step to blow. Stuart made a cigarette and offered the sack to Olaf.

"What happens now?" Olaf asked.

Stuart shrugged. "They'll have to figure that out between themselves. Maybe they'll make it up, but I doubt it. Milo will probably run Ernie off."

"Ernie ain't gonna like that."

Stuart laughed mirthlessly. "He won't have much choice."

"Then what? Ernie won't leave the country. More'n likely he'll throw in with that bunch down along the creek."

"If he does, Milo will kill him."

It shocked him to hear himself speak those words so

91

emotionlessly. Yet he knew they were true. Milo's inherent violence had at last reached the point of no return. Nor was Ernie any better. No. Ernie was a hell of a sight worse.

He got up wearily. "Come on. Let's lug Ernie in."

He clumped down the stairs with Olaf close behind. Ernie still lay in the buggy, curled up and breathing harshly. Stuart dragged him out, and together they carried him inside. They did not carry him upstairs to bed. That was a dignity Stuart didn't owe him. Instead they dumped him on the horsehair sofa in the living room.

Olaf headed for the door. Stuart called, "Go to bed, Olaf. Send somebody else down to the fence to take your place."

"All right, Stu. Thanks." The door closed.

Now that it was over, Stuart felt the full toll the night's strain had taken of his strength. He climbed the stairs to his room and flopped, fully dressed, on the rumpled bed.

Still, it took a while for him to go to sleep. Tension didn't slacken just because you wanted it to.

Nothing but disaster could result from the fight tonight. And Nora Dykes had won.

He was not aware of sleep, nor could he have said what awakened him. But an odd spasm of uneasiness shook him the moment he opened his eyes.

The sun was just coming up in the east. Outside, roosters were crowing, and probably had been for some time. The house was like a tomb. Stuart lay utterly still for a couple of minutes, listening. He heard no sound inside the house.

He swung his legs over the side of the bed, feeling as though he hadn't slept at all. And then he began to remember all that had happened last night.

Hell, both Milo and Ernie ought to be awake by now.

He got to his feet. He ran a hand through his hair and grabbed his hat from the bedpost. He stumbled into the hall.

Downstairs all was still. Stuart wondered if Ernie still lay sleeping on the couch. He walked down the hall toward his father's room. Maybe he could talk some sense into the old man. Maybe this morning, Milo would simply admit that Nora had made jackasses out of both him and Ernie and laugh it off. If he could do that, disaster might still be averted.

But Stuart didn't really believe it could. He knew both Milo and Ernie too well. Neither had enough of a sense of humor to be able to laugh at himself.

He opened the door of Milo's room and stepped inside.

Milo lay curled up, half on his stomach, half on his side. His face was toward the wall.

An odd, cold sensation crept down Stuart's spine. Something was . . . not right about the way Milo lay. He didn't move.

He crossed the room in three strides. He seized his father's shoulder and rolled him onto his back.

He saw, then. He saw Milo's blank eyes, the slack way his mouth hung open. He saw the hilt of the butcher knife protruding from the center of Milo's chest and the pool of blood on the bed where he had lain . . .

93

For a long time—it seemed a long time—he stared at Milo in shocked unbelief. It wasn't possible! Milo had been a giant—invincible, indestructible.

He still looked big, but now he was inert, like any dead thing. His personality, his ruthlessness, his power these things were gone.

An overpowering sense of loss struck Stuart. He had fought with Milo, disagreed with him, opposed him, but he had loved him too. He had remembered, through all the bad years while Milo changed and became hard, what Milo had been like in the early years.

Now it was over. He would never understand the forces that had changed his father.

He moved, having the feeling he had stood here thus for hours. He walked slowly to the door, almost as if he were walking in his sleep.

He moved along the hall and walked slowly down the stairs. He could kill Ernie now. He *would* kill Ernie, without mercy, the instant he saw him.

His eyes went to the horsehair sofa immediately, but Ernie wasn't there. There was only the indentation of his heavy body.

The kitchen was empty. So was the yard. But smoke was rising from the rusty tin chimney of the bunkhouse.

Stuart crossed the yard. His mind was sick. He wondered if Nora had guessed that her plan would breed murder. He wondered if she even cared.

The door to the bunkhouse was open. From the connecting cookshack issued the smell of boiling coffee— and flapjacks—and steak. The smells, which usually stimulated Stuart's appetite, this morning only formed a tight knot of nausea in his stomach.

Those of the crew who were not on top riding, were sitting at the long table that ran down the center of the bunkhouse. There were five or six. Stuart didn't pay much attention. Olaf Gurtler was among them.

Olaf glanced up, saw Stuart's face, and stepped back over the bench. Rounding the table, he asked worriedly, "What's the matter? You look—"

"The old man's dead," Stuart said. "Milo's dead."

Even hearing the words spoken by his own lips, he could scarcely believe them. This was some kind of nightmare—or seemed so. The men were all up now, crowding around him, amazement and unbelief in their eyes and voices. "How Stu? When? I can't believe it! Not Milo!"

"A butcher knife in the chest," Stuart said bitterly. "While he slept. He never even had a chance to defend himself."

He could see Ernie now, see that unclean look of pleasure on Ernie's face as he crept up the stairs in early morning clutching the kitchen knife in his powerful hand. He shuddered.

Olaf said, "Ernie?"

"Who else?"

"Where is he? Still in the house?"

Stuart shook his head. "If he'd been in the house, he'd be dead now too. No, he's gone. Didn't anybody see him leave?"

The men shook their heads. Stuart tried to think clearly, to decide what must be done. It was all on him today. Stuart Post was Skull.

CHAPTER TEN

They poured out of the bunkhouse, their breakfast forgotten, and streamed into the house. Stuart didn't try to stop them. Milo Post had been something more than a mere man for so many years that they found it all but impossible to believe he was dead. They had to see for themselves.

Waiting in the sunwashed yard, Stuart tried to plan his course. First, he must send for the sheriff. He must try and discover where Ernie had gone. If he could figure out which horse Ernie had ridden he might be able to pick up some trail . . .

The men came out of the house. Their faces were sober, stiff with awe.

Stuart rolled a cigarette with hands surprisingly steady under the circumstances. He said, "Olaf, make him a coffin. Take all day if you need to, but make a good one."

"Sure, Stu. Sure. I'll get right at it." Olaf headed for the blacksmith shop.

"Now," Stuart said, "I want three of you to go down and relieve the guard on the fence."

They looked at each other uncertainly. After a bit of shuttling about, three of them moved away toward the corral.

Two were left. Duke Revel and Phil Armstrong. Stuart said, "Duke, find out which horse Ernie took. Phil, head for town and get the sheriff. Keep your mouth shut. Tell the sheriff Milo is dead, but don't tell anybody else. Understand?"

Phil nodded and moved away. Duke trailed him. Stuart watched them, feeling weighted with all the responsibility that had suddenly been thrust upon him. He had inherited, along with Skull, all the hatreds, conflicts and trouble fostered by Milo's and Ernie's ruthless actions. When the people of the country, particularly those below Skull's fence, found out that Milo was dead and Ernie gone, they would use the opportunity to good advantage. Probably they'd move against Skull at once and in force.

Stuart crossed the dusty yard and sat down on the stoop in front of the back door. The shock of Milo's death was still with him. He scowled at the bare ground. All this trouble had been born the day Milo hanged Hugh Shore. Had it not been for that, Milo would still be alive.

Duke left the corral and crossed the yard to him.

"He took that big blaze-faced sorrel, Stu. The one with the stockings. He shouldn't be hard to trail on that one. Olaf trimmed his hoofs less than a week ago."

Stuart got up. "All right. Let's go." He walked toward the corral, with Duke following close behind. He could hear Olaf sawing in the blacksmith shop.

He roped out a horse. So did Duke. He flung up his saddle, cinched it down and mounted. Duke closed the corral gate behind them.

Stuart didn't intend to track Ernie right now. He had to be here when the sheriff arrived, and he would rather leave the capture of Ernie to the sheriff and a posse anyway. But he did want to ascertain the direction Ernie had taken. He wanted to be sure Ernie had really gone—that he wasn't skulking around out in the brush somewhere.

He headed up the lane, not even bothering to watch the ground for sign. At the road he said, "You go left, Duke. I'll go right. Ride about a mile along the road, then cut toward the rims. Stay on soft ground. I'll meet you."

He turned right and urged his horse to a trot. He figured Ernie would go out on top first thing. There were thousands of acres up there, covered with timber, heavy brush and aspen thickets. Ernie knew the plateau top as well as the old man had, and could hide out up there for two of three days until he decided what to do.

Ernie must be both panicky and uncertain. He had committed one of the worst crimes known to man. He would want time to think and plan.

After he had gone about a mile, Stuart swung left up through the cedars. He kept his eyes on the ground and rode at a walk. Sun beat down through the scattered cedars, laying a dappled pattern on the earth. Dust arose from the hoofs of Stuart's horse. The smell of cedars and sage was pungent and pleasant.

Down below, the house seemed to be resting peacefully in the morning sun. It was hard to believe that Milo lay stiff and cold in one of its rooms, and that his death would affect the whole county.

The hayfields were turning brown, but they had a lush look to them that said they had not suffered for lack of water. In one field, far up the valley, Stuart could see the shine of irrigation water spreading across it. He could see the irrigator's horse, standing saddled with reins trailing. That was probably Quinn. He must have left the bunkhouse early, before Stuart discovered Milo's body.

His horse climbed steadily, strongly, through the rolling cedar hills that footed the precipitous rim. Half an hour passed.

And then Stuart found them: tracks of a horse being urged uphill at a lunging gallop.

He dismounted and examined the sign. From the complete dryness of the prints, he judged they had been made an hour, maybe two hours before.

As he knelt there, he heard hoofbeats. He went tense, then relaxed when he saw Duke.

"Find 'em?" Duke asked.

"I think so. Follow these and go all the way up to where the trail starts. If they take the trail, come back to the house. If they don't—well, come back to the house anyway. I don't want you getting killed."

Duke said, "It's him all right. It's that blaze-faced sorrel. I can tell by the prints."

Stuart nodded. He rose, climbed his horse and reined him back toward the house.

There had been little doubt in his mind, before, that Ernie had killed Milo. Now there was none. Brother or no brother, Ernie deserved only death—by a bullet or by hanging.

The hours of waiting passed with maddening slowness. Duke returned with the news that Ernie had taken the rimrock trail. Just knowing that made Stuart breathe a little easier. He could be reasonably sure that Ernie would constitute no problem, at least for today. Nor was there much chance that Ernie would get away. No. He'd stay in the country, all right, as handy as possible to Skull. He wouldn't abandon his inheritance if he could help it.

Ernie had the same delusion Milo had possessed—that he was above the law. His thinking would lead him to one inevitable conclusion: he had gotten away with hanging Hugh Shore; he could get away with this as well.

Only he couldn't. The evidence against him was overwhelming. And he had practically confessed when he ran away.

Knowing Ernie, Stuart could count on one other thing. When Ernie realized, at last, that there was no way out—that Skull was lost and only death awaited him—he would become extremely dangerous. Without scruples, without pity, enjoying the infliction of pain, he might strike anywhere, commit any violent act. Beyond doubt he would do something—maybe something more terrible than the crime he had already done.

The sheriff rode up the lane in mid-morning, and stepped down by the back door. Stuart was in the kitchen, sipping coffee.

Mountain came in, tipped back his hat and wiped his streaming face with a bandanna. "Hot," he said. "And getting hotter."

Stuart got a cup and poured him coffee. Dan sat

down across the table and sipped it. "So Milo's dead."

There was something strange in the way he said it. Stuart had the obscure impression that he was pleased. He said, "Yes, he's dead."

"Who did it?"

"That's your job, isn't it? To find out?"

"Don't get proddy, Stu. Where's Ernie?"

"Gone. Phil told you that, didn't he?"

"Uh-huh. Phil said Ernie did it."

"He probably did. He and the old man fought last night."

"Over Nora Dykes?"

Stuart nodded. Again he had a feeling about the sheriff's attitude. It was different, somehow, than it had been before.

He could guess what had caused the change. Milo and Ernie Post had been the strength of Skull. Now both of them were gone. Dan Mountain knew their going meant changes.

"The Lord moves in mysterious ways," Dan Mountain intoned. "Something like this was long overdue, the way Milo was going."

Stuart grunted sourly. "Maybe so, but I wouldn't count on the Lord to do *your* job for you. You know Ernie as well as I do. Brother or no brother, he's nothing but an animal. If he thinks he's cornered—"

"He's not your brother," Dan Mountain said.

"What? What the hell are you talking about?"

"You mean you didn't know?"

"Know what?"

"Well I'll be damned!" Mountain scowled incredulously at him. Then he said, "Twenty-five years ago, Milo was just about alone in this part of the country. Brought in his wife and settled where Skull is now. I guess that's why nobody knew about Ernie—and by the time people started settling, they just took it for granted he was Milo's boy. But he wasn't. Milo got to figuring he wasn't going to have a son to carry on after he was gone so one time he brought Ernie home with him from Denver. Picked him off a freight. Ernie wasn't no more than seven or eight."

Stuart's mind was numb. He heard himself saying, "But why didn't he tell me?"

Mountain's face had lost some of its harshness. "Your ma was kind of a frail woman, an' Milo broke her. Maybe he didn't mean to an' maybe the country had somethin' to do with it. But he was afraid you'd be like her—wouldn't be tough enough to hold Skull together. He'd have left half of Skull to Ernie—or at least a good share of it—if he'd died a normal death. I guess he wanted you to think Ernie was your brother, so you'd try to be more like him."

Stuart stared at him wordlessly. Yet he knew that all this must be true. He'd suspected it. He'd always suspected it. A sudden, vast relief came over him. Dan Mountain had just explained why he and Ernie were so different.

"Skull's yours now," the sheriff said. "And I'd just as well tell you, Milo wasn't the only one who didn't think you were tough enough to hold it together the way he did."

"Maybe I'm not," Stuart said slowly, "if it means

102

hanging everybody who helps himself to a few beeves."

Mountain eked out a thin smile. "That bunch down the creek—they were scared of Milo and Ernie. They ain't scared of you. My advice would be to give them what they want."

"And what *do* they want?"

"A little water. A little graze. You've got too damn much of both. You could spare them some."

"And save you a peck of trouble. That it?"

"Maybe. Why not?"

Stuart eyed him narrowly. There was something very close to insolence in the sheriff's tone and manner. Maybe he, too, thought Stuart was soft. All right. He was too soft to do the things Milo had done. But by God he wasn't too soft to hold onto what was his. And he never would be.

He stood up. "I'll tell you why not! Because they wouldn't be satisfied with a little water—or a little graze." He emphasized the words savagely. "What kind of sandy are you trying to run on me, Dan? You know damned good and well if I give them anything now they'll think it's because I'm scared."

"Not if I talked to them first."

Stuart waited, suspicious and on guard.

"It's the smart thing to do," Mountain said persuasively. "You know it is. I've got to go after Ernie. I might have to chase him a hundred miles. I might be gone a week. A lot can happen in a week and I wouldn't be here to stop it."

Stuart thought it over. His own inclination was to

right some of the wrongs his father and Ernie had perpetrated. Skull didn't need the entire creek.

Besides that, the small ranchers below Skull's boundary were itching for trouble. Only fear had held them back. With Milo and Ernie gone they would not be so afraid.

By releasing creek water, Stuart could immobilize them for two or three days. Having been without water so long, needing it so desperately, they wouldn't let it flow on past. They'd get out in their hayfields and irrigate. And while they were doing that, they wouldn't be making trouble for Skull.

He said, "All right. Talk to them. I'll play it your way first. I'll turn water back into the creek. I'll pay them for the cattle Milo killed. If they don't start pushing, maybe later we can talk about graze. But if they do—I'm warning you, Dan—they'll get the same treatment from me that they'd have gotten from Milo."

The sheriff grinned. "Fair enough." He finished his coffee and got to his feet. "I want to see Milo."

Stuart led him up the stairs to Milo's room. The sheriff poked around the room, then crossed and looked at Milo. He pulled the knife callously from Milo's chest.

"This one of yours?"

"It's one of the kitchen knives."

"You think anyone else could have got in here?"

Stuart shook his head. "There was a guard on the fence all night. Ernie had passed out on the living room couch. Uh-uh. Maybe it could have been done, but nobody would have had the guts to try. Besides, if it

104

had been an outsider he'd have killed Ernie first."

"Guess you're right." The sheriff turned to go. "I need a posse. How many of your men can you let me have?"

Stuart studied Dan Mountain closely. First, the sheriff was conveniently getting himself out of the country after warning Stuart he might be gone a week. Second, he was trying to recruit a posse from among Skull's riders . . .

"Not a damned one," Stuart said. "You get your posse in town. I need every man I've got."

A show of force was the only chance he had. Maybe even that wasn't going to be enough.

CHAPTER ELEVEN

Stuart stood on the stoop and watched the sheriff ride out. From the blacksmith shop came the echoing pound of a hammer as Olaf worked steadily on Milo's casket.

Stuart rolled a smoke, lit it, then crossed to his horse. He mounted and rode toward the creek. When he reached it, he turned into it, heading upstream.

There was no doubt in his mind about the wisdom of this course. This wasn't weakness; it was expediency. Men busy irrigating with much needed water hadn't time for making trouble.

The rest of it—well, he didn't know. It was right and just that Skull pay the lower valley ranchers for the cattle Milo had killed. But was now the time? Wouldn't it be construed as weakness and fear?

He supposed it would. But he intended to try it anyway. If Skull was ever going to get along with its neighbors, it had to start someplace.

He splashed along upstream in the shallow trickle that had raised in the stream bed below the dam. A mile or so below the house, another dam took even this small amount of water out of the stream. But he could get that on his way downcountry.

A deer spooked from his approach, a doe, and ran up out of the stream bed to cross the hayfield, her fawn gamboling along at her heels. Trees laid a dappled shade on the water and on the rocky bed of the stream. The air here was cool, made so by the trees and the damp bed of the creek.

From this point, Stuart stared up at the dam. Built of logs and brush, it towered nearly fifty feet in the air. He put his horse into the trail leading up and a minute or so later came out at the top beside the concrete headgate of Skull's upper ditch.

He dismounted and let the reins of his horse trail. He went over to the headgate and turned the big iron wheel.

The headgate began to drop on its worm gear. The level of water behind it began to rise and the level in the ditch began to fall.

It took Stuart several minutes to lower it all the way down. When he finished water was spilling over the mossy, dark-colored logs to the rocks below. It made a pleasant, soothing sound. Spray rose nearly to the top of the dam and the sun struck iridescent colors from the spray.

Stuart stepped back into the saddle. He rode out into the hayfield until he spotted the irrigator working near his grazing horse.

Stuart rode to him and sat looking down. "Go on back to the house, Quinn. I've turned the creek loose."

Quinn tipped back his hat. He was about fifty-five, and the best irrigator Skull had. He'd been a cowboy since the age of twelve. He squinted at Stuart and said, "Milo won't like it, Stu."

"Milo's dead."

"Dead?" Pure amazement made Quinn's voice squeak.

"That's right. He and Ernie had a fight last night down at Nora's place. I guess you knew about that. When I got up this morning I found Milo with a knife in his chest and Ernie gone."

Quinn eyed Stuart with growing respect. "An' you figure the water will keep that bunch downstream busy until you get set?"

Stuart nodded.

Quinn grinned with approval. He walked to his horse and mounted. He fell in behind Stuart and they rode downcountry toward the house, little more than a speck in the distance.

It would be mid-afternoon before the water reached the ranches below Skull. The near dry stream bed would soak up a lot of it as it traveled along. Stuart had turned it all back for this very reason. He wanted them to get the water as soon as possible. They wouldn't stay ignorant of Milo's death for long. Probably they already knew.

He passed the house without stopping, and Quinn left him at the lane. He rode on downcountry until he reached the lower dam and here, again, he closed the headgate. Then he cut up to the road and rode toward the lower fence.

Noon came and passed. He reached the fence at about one, found the men there alert, and went on through.

A new, peculiar kind of uneasiness was growing in him. Despite the warmth of the sun and the beauty of the day, it seemed as though an ominous grayness hung over the land.

Stuart knew what caused it. He didn't really believe he could reason with Skull's neighbors. Hatred and outrage had been building up too long to be smoothed over now. The culmination of it all had been the hanging of Hugh Shore and the killing of the cattle.

No. The water might keep them busy for a day or two. But their hatred went too deep to be destroyed by righting the injustice that had caused it.

There would be more fighting, more dying.

Stuart shook his head gloomily, but he rode on and shortly thereafter turned into the little twisting road that led to Nora's house.

Somewhat warily, he stepped down before the door. It was open, and his feet scarcely touched the ground before Katie stood framed in it.

Her face was pale, drawn. Her eyes were red, probably both from weeping and from sleeplessness. She said lifelessly, "Hello, Stuart."

He gazed steadily at her. She was less pretty this

morning, yet she was more desirable than ever before. Pity stirred in him. He took a step toward her, and suddenly she came running. His arms closed around her tightly. Her body shook as though from a chill. Then tears burst forth like a summer storm.

He held her all the time she was crying, patting her back with awkward sympathy. When she could talk, she pulled away, wiping at her streaming eyes and cheeks with the back of her hand. "Stuart, I'm sorry. I'm awfully sorry."

"About Milo? Then you've heard?"

"The sheriff stopped by."

Stuart glanced worriedly toward the house. "How's your mother taking it?"

"She's ashamed. She's terribly ashamed. She blames herself for his death."

"I want to see her."

"Stuart, not now, please. I know you must be bitter and I don't blame you. But don't—"

"No, Katie. If I'm bitter, it's against Ernie, not against her. She couldn't have had any idea he would kill Milo."

"She didn't. I know she didn't! She meant to turn them against each other but she didn't want it to go this far."

"Let me see her, Katie." Stuart said gently.

"All right. Come on in. I'll make some coffee. Have you eaten?"

He shook his head and followed her toward the door. "I suppose Dan stopped and told everybody along the creek that Milo was dead."

"I don't know. I suppose he did."

Stuart stepped into the house.

Nora sat at the table, her head buried in her arms. She looked up as he came in. Her face was haggard, her eyes dull with pain.

"I didn't mean for either of them to die, Stuart."

"I know."

"I wish I were dead. I'm not fit to live." She began to cry again.

Stuart was acutely embarrassed, but he managed to say, "What's done is done, Nora. Blaming yourself isn't going to change things. If Milo hadn't—" He couldn't go on. He'd meant to say that if Milo hadn't hanged Hugh Shore, this wouldn't have happened. And it wouldn't. But it seemed disloyal to blame Milo for anything now. It was better forgotten. He tried a new approach.

"Have you any idea how many cattle you lost that day, Nora?"

"No. Why?"

"Because I want to pay you for them."

She stared at him suspiciously. "Why?"

Katie must have heard, for she appeared abruptly in the kitchen door. Her attitude didn't match Nora's, but obviously she was waiting for an explanation.

"Don't look at me that way, either of you," Stuart said impatiently. "I thought it was wrong when Milo killed those cattle. Only then I couldn't do anything about it. Now I can. That's all there is to it."

"Are you going to pay the others?" Nora demanded.

"Of course I am."

She watched him for a moment more. Katie returned to the kitchen, apparently satisfied. Stuart knew what Nora was thinking, that by offering to pay her for the cattle he was trying to buy something. She figured that since he'd become boss of Skull, he'd changed his mind about marrying Katie, and wanted her.

He said bluntly, "Haven't you ever known any decent men?"

She flushed deeply and her glance dropped. In a barely audible voice she said, "Yes. But no many of the other kind. And you're—"

"I'm a Post. Is that it?"

"I guess so. I'm sorry, Stuart."

"You can relax," he said harshly. "I still want to marry Katie. Now how about the cattle? How many were there?"

"Grady Rifkin said fourteen."

"Thirty dollars a head all right?"

"Of course. That's more than generous, Stuart. As thin as they were, they weren't worth that."

"You'd rather refuse, wouldn't you?"

She looked up, a glint of panic in her eyes. But she nodded with reluctant honesty.

He said, "I'm not giving you anything. I owe you for the cattle. You're not obligated to me."

"All right, Stuart."

He sat down and pulled a checkbook from his pocket. He wrote out the check swiftly with a pen that was on the table. He handed it to Nora. "Will you let me do you a favor now? Because I want to?"

She hesitated, then nodded.

"You and Katie gather up your cattle. Push them through our fence. They can run on Skull the rest of the year."

Nora didn't reply immediately.

"Getting out—working—will be good for both of you, Nora. Will you do it?"

Still Nora hesitated.

"Damn it, Nora! Katie promised to marry me before this ever happened. We were going away today. Maybe we can't get married right away, but that doesn't mean . . . Well, hell, I'm going to be one of your family, Nora. You'd just as well start getting used to the idea. Why can't I do something for you if I want to?"

She smiled wanly. "I guess you can. Thank you, Stuart."

"All right," he said, flushing faintly. "You can make this place pay, Nora. You can be independent and live on it and make it pay."

She refused to meet his eyes, knowing what he was trying to say. She just nodded silently.

He didn't know whether Nora really could change her way of life or not. He wasn't sure that she even wanted to. But if she did want to, she'd have the opportunity now. It was up to her.

Katie came in, bearing a plate of fried eggs and ham and a steaming pot of coffee. She set them down before Stuart.

"Sit down and have a cup of coffee with me," he said.

She sat down meekly, anxiously.

"What's going to happen, Stuart?"

112

He began to eat. He discovered that he was hungry now. The image of Milo's body had faded from his mind. He sipped the hot coffee gratefully. He sighed because Katie was still waiting.

"I don't know," he said.

"Milo's death and Ernie's running away will change things. The men below here—"

"Won't be afraid any more. I know."

"I didn't mean it that way. Milo and Ernie—"

He smiled at her. "Katie, it's all right." He knew what she had been trying to say. The same thought would be in the mind of every man in the county, from those directly below here to the far-flung ranches that bordered on the farthest boundaries of Skull. The two giants who had held this empire of cattle and grass were gone. Only Stuart remained—Stuart, who lacked the implacable ruthlessness that had made Milo and Ernie seem so formidable. Stuart, who might possibly be bluffed, or scared.

Katie's eyes devoured his face. "Stuart, take me away, just like we planned. I'm afraid . . . that something is going to happen to you."

"And let them have it by default? Don't you know me better than that, Katie?"

"Oh, dear," she said. "I didn't think you would."

Stuart finished his breakfast and got up. Katie came to the door with him. Outside, she stood on tiptoe to kiss him on the mouth.

"Be careful, Stuart. Please be careful. So many men hated your father, and now they'll take all that out on you—"

He pulled her against him hungrily. For the first time since he'd known her she responded with equal passion.

He didn't know how things would turn out. He didn't know how long the fight would last. But he did know this: he had something to fight for now. Katie. Skull. He loved them both and they were his to hold. All his, and his alone. What happened from now on was strictly up to Stuart Post himself.

CHAPTER TWELVE

Leaving Nora's place, Stuart rode upcountry until he was out of sight. Then he swung around, rode through the brush until he struck the road below the house, and continued on toward town.

He knew fully the risks he took. Riding into Grady Rifkin's place alone, even riding this road alone, was dangerous. The smart thing, the cautious, sensible thing, would be to ride this errand in the company of half a dozen Skull riders.

Yet he wasn't doing it this way without reason. Riding in company with several Skull riders might be safer. But it would also tell them he was afraid.

He rode straight in the saddle, his right hand hanging loosely at his side, thumb touching the saddle skirt, cavalry fashion. He kept his eyes straight ahead and his body relaxed, as though this were nothing more than a casual trip to town for the mail.

Rifkin's place was less than a mile below Nora's. It lay across the dry creek at the mouth of a little ravine.

Rifkin was one of the lucky ones. That ravine held a spring that ran even in dry years. He had piped it down past the house. At the house it spilled out of the pipe into a ditch that carried it on down to an earthen stock tank beside the corrals.

The house was small, a two-room affair built of hand-squared logs chinked with concrete. The yard was bare ground, its starkness relieved by scattered farm machinery, a few idly scratching White Leghorn chickens, and a white wisp of woodsmoke before the door. Rifkin's wife, Susan, was out beside the house hanging clothes from a single, sagging line. The only green things visible were the vegetables growing in her tiny garden patch, which she watered with buckets carried from the stock tank.

The number of saddle horses tied to the corral poles, four of them, warned Stuart to turn around and ride back. But he stubbornly continued, aware that he must have been seen, and unwilling to turn away no matter what the odds.

He could feel them watching him as his horse picked its careful way across the dry creek bed. He lifted the horse to a trot and rode up the slight grade into Rifkin's yard.

Susan Rifkin paused in her work to stare at him. Her face was lined, and pale today. Her eyes were scared. And yet, he seemed to sense another quality in her— that of satisfaction, even triumph. And the hatred was there too. Hatred for Skull, for anyone who bore the name of Post.

He nodded to her. "Where's Grady, Mrs. Rifkin?"

"Barn," she said, and turned back to her work.

Stuart rode toward the barn at a walk. They were all here, he guessed. Probably having a meeting to decide what they were going to do.

He reined up before the barn. The feeling of being watched was very tangible now, like an invisible wall through which he dared not ride. He reined up. "Grady! You there?"

The door creaked open, just enough to pass the body of a man.

Grady Rifkin was as big as Ernie Post. Older, his face was deeply seamed, his hair darkly gray. He wore run-over-at-the-heels cowman's work boots, dirty levis and a plaid flannel shirt, despite the heat. His tan, wide-brimmed Stetson was misshapen from years of hard usage, its brim pulled to a point before his eyes. Its crown above the band was black with sweat. His eyes were blue-gray, and hard as slate.

He spat tobacco juice at the feet of Stuart's horse.

"What the hell do *you* want?"

Stuart stifled his temper. He said, "I guess you've heard Milo's dead."

"I heard. If you expect me to say I'm sorry, you're barkin' up the wrong tree. I say good riddance."

Stuart shrugged. Knowing his face had reddened, knowing his eyes were glittering with anger, he said, "There'll be some changes made. For one thing, the whole creek is on its way down here right now. You can have it until you're through irrigating."

Rifkin glared at him suspiciously. "Kinda late for that. I doubt if we could get a hay crop now anyhow."

"You can get some. You can get one cutting, even if it won't be very high."

Rifkin did not soften. He spat again. Stuart's horse lifted its spattered hoof daintily and put it down with a hard stomp.

"Another thing," Stuart said. "Get me a tally of the cattle Milo killed. I'll pay for 'em."

The barn door creaked. Nick Stamm came out, followed by his son Wally. Behind Wally was Tim Boorom and Vince Doyle.

Wally sneered, "Changed your tune, haven't you?" He nodded significantly at his father and the others. "The son-of-a-bitch is scared, that's what!" He swung back toward Stuart. "Sure. We'll take the water and we'll take your money for the cattle. Maybe we'll take the whole damn shootin' match before we're through."

Stuart looked at Rifkin. "Is this punk doing your talking for you?"

Wally stepped clear of the others, falling into the tense stance that gunmen use. Stuart said. "Well, Rifkin, is this your place or isn't it? Am I talking to you or am I talking to that trigger-happy squirt?"

"You'll talk to all of us," Rifkin growled.

Wally hadn't moved. His hand hung like a claw over his gun in its pared-down holster. His face was tense, the cords standing out in his skinny neck. His mouth worked, twitching slightly at one corner.

Stuart had beaten him once, but that time Katie had distracted Wally by launching herself at him. This time there would be no distractions—except that as soon as either Wally or Stuart moved, the others

117

would buy into the fight too.

He stared at Wally. Wally might be a little crazy, but that made him all the more dangerous. And doubly so today because his friends were watching him.

Stuart kept his eyes on Wally's, beating them down by sheer force of will. Wally switched his eyes nervously away, and back again. Finally he settled it by fixing them on the Bull Durham tag dangling from Stuart's shirt pocket.

Stuart felt like a rabbit ringed by snakes. Wally was like a rattler that has been prodded with a stick. He'd made his brag, before these others whom he wanted to impress. He'd use that gun, one way or another, before Stuart left the yard. If Stuart turned to ride away, he'd get it in the back.

He had the sudden feeling that all these men had made their decisions. Stuart Post was closer to death than he had ever been before. They didn't intend to let him leave the yard alive.

A touchy moment, while Stuart's mind raced. Rifkin glared at him stolidly, unmoving. The others stood in a line against the door, waiting, tense and ready. Wally stood apart, still half-crouched. Except that now there was a different light in Wally's eyes. He also understood that decisions had been made. He understood that he had the backing of every man in the yard. The tiniest of smiles touched his thinned-out mouth.

Stuart had to break the deadlock before Wally's confidence built enough to crowd him into making his move.

Casually, as though these men's thoughts and intentions were unknown to him, he reined his horse around, toward Wally, halving the distance between them. To hold them steady, he said evenly, "Bring me your tallies. I'll give you a check."

As he came abreast of Wally and saw Wally start to step back, he flung his right leg over the saddle horn. Using his left foot in the stirrup for leverage, he dived from the saddle, straight at Wally Stamm.

Wally's hand streaked for his holster. The gun cleared just as Stuart struck.

Wally went back, trying to bring his gun to bear. Reflex made his finger tighten on the trigger, and the gun blasted prematurely.

Stuart didn't even try to use his own gun. Both his hands found Wally's wrist and twisted savagely.

Wally yelled and the gun slipped from his hand. More powerful, bigger than Wally, Stuart would soon have brought him under control. Before he had the chance, the others moved.

Nick Stamm was first. Seizing a shovel that leaned against the wall of the barn, he stepped in to the struggling pair. He waited warily and the instant he knew he could strike without hitting Wally, he swung.

Aimed at Stuart's head, the shovel missed and struck his shoulder instead. His whole right arm went numb and useless. Pain shot across his chest from the injured shoulder.

He wondered confusedly how smart he'd been. It had been certain that he would die from the moment he rode into Rifkin's yard. But was it better to be sledged

119

and beaten to death by half a dozen men than to be shot to death?

Stamm was standing back, trying for another swing. And Stuart, fighting with but one hand, was having difficulty now controlling the wiry, frantic Wally.

He had to keep Wally between himself and that shovel. He had to keep Stamm from swinging again.

Rifkin and the others were moving too, wanting a part of hurting a Post. Rifkin shouldered Stamm aside and swung a savage kick.

It struck Stuart's shoulder, the same shoulder the shovel had previously hurt. It toppled him and rolled him a full two yards, breaking his hold on Wally, tearing them apart.

Looking up, half blinded by pain, he saw their faces. Their lips were twisted, their teeth bared. Their eyes were bright and lusting.

Stuart came to his knees frantically and tried to make it to his feet. Stamm, plunged in, swinging the shovel again. Stuart ducked.

The shovel whistled past his head, no more than an inch above it. Stuart pushed against the ground with his good left arm, made it and staggered toward them.

Two were circling behind him. Rifkin met him head-on with a monstrous, sledging fist that crashed squarely into the middle of Stuart's face.

For an instant it seemed to him that he was facing Ernie again in one of the many brutal fights he'd had with him through the years that were past. His mind was foggy with the awful pain in his shoulder, numbed by the power behind that blow. He tried to focus his eyes on Rifkin, and fighting Ernie still in his mind, launched himself at the bigger man.

His fist slammed into Rifkin's bony, jutting jaw, sending spears of pain all the way to his shoulder. He tried to follow that blow with a right, but he'd gotten his injured arm no more than waist high when Rifkin's fist sank into his belly.

It doubled him, and as he pitched forward Rifkin sledged him on the neck with both hands clasped together.

Another man would have stayed down and died on the ground under the boots of the eager four that rushed in toward him. But Stuart had fought many a brutal, losing fight with Ernie. He didn't know how to stay down.

He rolled spasmodically, stunned and only half conscious. He brought his hands under him, and touched something . . .

It was the handle of a broken pitchfork. He seized it and fought his way up.

Two broken tines, and a broken handle. It blurred before his eyes. A manure fork, with several tines left. Enough to put the fear of God into this bunch.

Crouched like a wounded bear, he faced them, watching warily as Wally and Boorom tried to circle behind him. The elder Stamm still held the shovel. He growled, "Lemme at him. I'll knock that out of his hands quick enough."

He came lunging in, swinging the shovel. Stuart didn't try to parry the blow, knowing full well that the force of the swinging shovel would tear the fork from his weakened hands.

Instead he ducked, waited until the shovel whistled past, then lunged at Stamm.

Even now, decency was a part of him he could not ignore. He could have plunged the fork into Stamm's belly. Instead he dropped it slightly and jabbed it into Nick Stamm's thigh.

Stamm howled. Half turned and still turning, carried on by the shovel's momentum, his leg gave beneath him. The flesh, binding the fork, held it and yanked its shortened handle from Stuart's hands.

Now this had gone too far to end in anything but death. Stuart realized this and shot a hand toward his gun. His hand encountered only the empty holster.

Then they were on him, like a howling mob, all striking at once in an almost frenzied way.

Blows rained into Stuart's face, on his head, in his belly, and though some glanced harmlessly off arms and shoulders and chest, the combined force of those that did strike vital areas quickly put him on the ground.

They stood around him then, kicking as though at a stunned and vicious dog.

Human flesh couldn't stand much more. Unconsciousness reached for Stuart's senses. He'd die here in Rifkin's dirty yard, for no good reason, for no reason at all except the hate they had borne Milo and Ernie Post.

He tried to roll, to protect himself, but he found he couldn't move. Sun beat mercilessly into his face. A cloud of dust arose . . .

Dimly he heard a shrill screaming—a woman's voice. He tried to concentrate on the words but couldn't make them out.

Then the kicking stopped. For an instant, Stuart couldn't believe it. He turned his head weakly and saw Susan Rifkin standing there holding a double-barreled shotgun.

"I'll kill the lot of you if you touch him again! What kind of men are you? I don't like the Posts any better than you do, but I wouldn't let you treat a dog this way!"

Stuart put forth a monstrous effort of will. He got to his hands and knees. This way, he raised his head. He said with numb stubbornness, "Bring me your tallies and I'll write you a check."

CHAPTER THIRTEEN

They loaded him on his horse and tied his feet under the horse's belly so that he could not fall off. Rifkin gave his horse a cut on the rump with a quirt and the animal galloped out of the yard, taking the road toward Skull.

Stuart was lucky. He knew that. Except for some unexpected thread of decency in Susan Rifkin, he would now be lying dead back there, killed by their heavy boots. But in spite of this realization he was fighting mad. That bunch deserved no consideration. They were as brutal, as savage as wolves, and like wolves, they deserved only extermination. Milo had been right. You had to be hard—harder than those who would gobble you up—if you wanted to survive.

His hat was gone. His face was covered with blood and sweat and dust. His body was one great ache and every movement was pure torture, even after the horse slowed to a walk.

He thought of Wally Stamm, of Wally's father Nick. It would be a long time before Nick was up and around again. That pitchfork had been filthy, and had penetrated two inches or more into Stamm's thigh. If he didn't get to a doctor fast, gangrene would take his leg.

He was sorry about that, surprisingly enough. He wouldn't have minded killing Stamm, or hurting him with anything else. But a filthy manure fork . . .

He blacked out for a time and came to again as his horse was passing Nora's lane. He seized the reins and turned the animal toward her house. He couldn't make it to Skull. He couldn't even make it to the fence.

Riding in, he heard the pleasant, soothing sound of the creek running down past Nora's house. Rifkin and the others would have their water soon if they didn't have it now. He'd gained the time he had to have. There wasn't a man below here who would be able to let that water run on by.

He rode in to Nora's house and halted his horse before the door. He couldn't dismount. He couldn't even fall out of the saddle because his feet were tied beneath the horse's belly.

He felt weak and helpless, and the feeling only served to increase the anger that smoldered in his heart. Damn them!

He tried to call for Katie, but only a croak issued

from his throat. He started to turn his horse away, and then he heard her. Katie. Katie, seeing him and crying out.

Nora was right behind her. Nora steadied him while Katie ran inside for a knife. Katie cut the cord from his ankles and he slid left out of the saddle.

He was too big for them to catch, but they broke his fall and afterwards half carried, half dragged him inside the house.

He felt a cool, wet cloth on his face. He felt his shirt loosened and opened. One of them raised his head and he felt the acrid bite of whisky in his mouth.

He gagged, choked, but he swallowed most of what they'd given him. It coursed down his throat, leaving it warm, and lay in his stomach like suddenly gulped, scalding coffee.

Then it began to react, lessening his pain, reviving him, lightening the blackness of coma. He opened his eyes.

"Who did this to you?" Katie asked. "Who, Stuart?"

Stuart made a painful grin. "Your neighbors."

"Why? For heaven's sake, *why*?"

Stuart shrugged, and his face twisted with pain at the movement.

"What did you do?"

"Gave them water. Offered to pay for the cattle they'd lost."

He made a determined effort, and sat up on the couch they'd laid him on. Katie offered him a glass partly full of whisky and he gulped it down. He coughed from its bite in his throat.

Katie's voice was filled with outrage. "What's the matter with the men in this country?"

"They're hungry, Katie. They've got their backs to the wall."

"But you offered—"

"It's too late. It should have been done years ago."

"Will they accept your offer?"

"I don't know. I'll just have to wait and see." His eyes were heavy, his body exhausted. He could not remember ever having been so tired—or sore, though some of the beatings he'd taken at Ernie's hands had been nearly as bad as this.

He made himself stand up.

"Thanks." He grinned wryly. "I'd never have made it home." He limped toward the door. Katie came with him. At the door he paused.

"I wish you and Nora would go to town until this is over. Or come to Skull."

"No one will hurt us, Stuart."

"Don't be too sure. When that bunch down there strikes out, they won't care who they hurt."

"We'll be all right."

His knees began to shake. He was too weak to argue with her. He stumbled to his horse and heaved himself into the saddle. He grinned at Katie shakily and rode out.

Maybe, now that Rifkin and the others had worked out their anger on him, they'd be more reasonable. He could only wait and see. If they weren't . . . if they wanted a fight . . . well, there was enough of Milo in him to accommodate them in that respect.

Down there a while ago he'd been furiously angry. He'd wanted to exterminate Rifkin and his friends. Now, however he fought against it, his essential reasonableness returned.

That was the hell of it—he could always see the other side of any controversy. In this way he was different from Milo, different from Ernie. They'd only been able to see their own.

At the fence, the man on guard stared at Stuart as though he were a ghost. "Godalmighty! What happened to you?"

"Run-in with Rifkin and his friends. Rifkin may be coming through after a while. Pass him, but keep whoever's with him here."

"Sure." The man was still curious, but he didn't question Stuart further. Stuart lifted his horse to a lope, gritting his teeth against the pain in his battered body, and rode toward home.

He had the discouraged conviction that the odds against him were mounting. Not one of the lower valley ranchers really wanted to talk peace. Ernie was still loose, somewhere, capable of causing more trouble than all the lower valley ranchers combined. Nor would the sheriff be much help.

If the odds got too big, Stuart probably wouldn't be able to count on his crew, either.

He forced his mind away from its morbid train of thought. Whatever the odds, he'd still buck them. Maybe he'd lose, but it wouldn't be because he hadn't tried.

When he reached Skull, he slid out of his saddle beside the back door, unsaddled and turned the horse loose. He couldn't walk to the corral right now and he didn't feel like calling for help.

He flung saddle and bridle on the ground beside the door. He hobbled over to the pump. Here, he stripped the shredded shirt from his back and threw it on the ground.

He worked the pump handle until a stream gushed from the spout. He ducked his head under, let the stream run on his neck a while, then flung handfuls of the icy water over his chest and back.

He toweled himself dry, feeling better already. A few hours' sleep and he'd be okay. Almost.

Olaf came from the barn and crossed to him. "It's finished, Stu. The coffin, I mean. Take a look and see if you think it's all right."

Stuart swung to face him, saw his start of surprise and explained quickly what had happened. Olaf scowled. "That bunch needs a damn good lesson. Let me take half a dozen men down there—"

"Milo tried lessons," Stuart said wearily. "It didn't work. Come on, let's see what you've done."

He followed Olaf to the blacksmith shop and inspected the coffin. It was well made, sanded carefully, and lined with black cloth. Olaf said, "I don't want to hurry things, but it's pretty hot."

"Sundown," Stuart said. "We'll bury him then."

He tramped across the yard and entered the house. He took a bucket of water and a couple of towels upstairs. He washed Milo and changed his clothes. He carried Milo down the stairs and laid him on the living room couch.

Then he tramped back upstairs. He lay face down across the bed and fell asleep.

Olaf Gurtler wakened him, as he had last night. Stuart blinked at him groggily.

"What is it?"

"That son-of-a-bitch Rifkin. He's down in the yard. Says you told him to come."

Stuart's mouth twisted. Beat a man damn near to death, then take his money. His estimate of Rifkin dropped by several degrees. He said, "Tell him I'll be right down."

He put on a clean shirt, washed his face and ran a comb through his hair. He found another hat and put it on. He went into Milo's room and took Milo's gun and belt from the bedpost. He strapped them on. Then he went downstairs.

Rifkin was waiting in the yard. The sun was low in the west.

Stuart fumbled for makings and rolled a smoke. He said, "One thing. You're sure as hell not short on guts."

Rifkin scowled uncomfortably. "Last thing you said was—"

"I know," Stuart interrupted impatiently. "I know. But how the hell would you have got the money if you'd kicked me to death down there?"

"We didn't. We wouldn't 've done that."

"The hell you wouldn't." Stuart grunted in disgust. "All right, let's see your bill."

Olaf stood watchfully a couple of steps behind him. Rifkin handed Stuart a paper. It was an old bill from the feed store in town. He turned it over.

He read it slowly, deliberately. As he did, his face reddened and his teeth clenched. Finally he said, "One hundred and fifty-one cattle at seventy-five dollars a head. Eleven thousand, four hundred and twenty dollars total. Rifkin your arithmetic's no better than the way you count and appraise. You don't seriously think I'm going to pay this, do you?"

"You said you would."

"If it was an honest bill I would."

"You accusin' me . . . ?"

Stuart stepped forward. He stuck his face close to Rifkin's. He said, "You're goddam right I am. In the first place, Milo didn't kill over forty-five cattle at the most. Fourteen of those were Nora's. That leaves thirty-one. At thirty dollars a head, that's just under a thousand dollars. You want more'n ten times that much. And you won't get it. By God, you'll fry in hell before you get a dime!"

"I figured you'd say that. All the Posts are lyin' sons of—" Stuart slapped him hard across the mouth. He stepped back.

Rifkin's face turned almost purple. His eyes were deadly.

A fierce exultation rose in Stuart. Now. He and Rifkin on even terms.

Rifkin took a step toward him, then stopped abruptly. He glanced sideways at Olaf.

Stuart said, "No interference, Olaf. From you or anyone else."

"All right, Stu. Take him!"

Stuart's eyes bored steadily on Rifkin's. Rifkin stood

it for a long moment, and then he looked at the ground.

"What's the matter?" Stuart demanded. "Need four or five men to back you up?"

Rifkin refused to raise his head. "I didn't come here to fight," he growled. "Are you gonna pay that bill or ain't you?"

"Want me to tell you what to do with that bill, Grady?" Rifkin looked up, then.

"I'll keep the bill," he muttered. "I'll make you wish you had paid it."

"What'll you do, Grady?"

"We'll take this ranch. The whole goddam thing, water, graze, hayfields."

"Start now, Grady. Take me."

Rifkin turned without replying and shuffled to his horse, a great bear of a man. He mounted heavily.

Stuart watched him ride out of the yard. He was sorry they'd tried to shove that crooked bill down his throat. He'd wanted to pay them for damage they'd sustained. He would still pay a proper bill. But they'd never give him one. Not now.

What would their next move be? He couldn't guess. But he did know they'd make one. They'd keep making them until Skull had its back to the wall. With a dozen men you couldn't guard all the far-flung borders of the ranch.

Nor were the lower valley ranchers the only threat. There was still Ernie, who could be counted upon to do something disastrously damaging. There were Skull's other neighbors, to north and west and south. The instant Grady and his friends succeeded at something they'd move in too.

There was one easy way they could pull Skull down unopposed. Thinking of it put a small chill in Stuart's spine. They could kill Stuart Post. Ernie was in no position to defend Skull. The sheriff wouldn't interfere since there were no heirs. Even if he did, his interference would be nominal and for appearances only.

Stuart would have to ride carefully from here on out. He would be watched, every place he rode. He would never know when a gun was pointed at his back.

He shook himself savagely. He turned to Olaf and said, "Get the men together and hitch up a buckboard. It's almost sundown now."

Olaf moved away.

CHAPTER FOURTEEN

The sun flamed orange and gold on the western rims as the little cavalcade wound its way from the house, down across the creek and up, then, through the cedars to the high knoll back of the house.

Stuart drove the buckboard with Milo's casket in the back. Skull's riders paced their mounts slowly beside and behind it.

At the crest of the knoll, Stuart pulled up and got shovels out of the buckboard bed. He broke ground at a spot from which he could look down and see the house, the outbuildings, and the vast hayfields of Skull. He didn't suppose a dead man cared where he was buried, and yet he knew he would like this spot himself. The air was clean up here. It was a lonely place, but it was also one from which all the activities of Skull could be observed.

He and Olaf dug steadily until the clouds faded to deep purple, and then turned their shovels over to a couple of others who quickly thereafter finished the digging in the soft, shaly ground.

With rope slings, they lowered the casket carefully into the grave. Stuart lighted a lantern, and while Olaf held it high, he read a few passages, marked long ago, from the family Bible. He closed the Book then and said softly, "All right. Fill it in."

He got to the seat of the buckboard and drove back down the steep slope toward the house alone. He supposed he should have held a regular funeral, with a minister officiating. But he hadn't wanted crowds of curious onlookers around. Nor had he wanted to risk letting crowds of hostile neighbors in on Skull.

Sadness was in him, mixed with regret. The way of Milo's dying had been unworthy of Milo as a man. Milo had built this flourishing ranch out of little more than sheer determination. He should have died like the giant he was, for a worthy reason.

Stuart drove slowly to the barn. He got down, unhitched the team and led them inside. He removed the harness from both horses and hung it on its pegs against the wall. Then he led the horses to the corral and put them inside.

At loose ends, he wandered aimlessly around the yard, trying to anticipate where Rifkin and the others would strike first. The crew filtered into the yard singly and in small groups. They put their horses away and retired to the bunkhouse.

Olaf Gurtler, closer than any of the others to Stuart, crossed the yard, saw him sitting on the stoop by the back door, and sat down with him. Silently Gurtler rolled a smoke and offered the sack to Stuart.

They smoked in silence, their cigarette ends glowing coals in the darkness. At last Gurtler said, "Got it figured out?"

Stuart shook his head. "I doubt if anybody could figure an unpredictable bunch like that one down there. But I'd guess offhand that their best bet would be to get rid of me."

"That's the way I figure it. No more dumb stunts like you riding down to Rifkin's place alone. You take some of us with you, wherever you go."

Stuart tried to make out Olaf's face in the dark.

"The going may get rough," he said. "Will the crew stick?"

"Some of 'em will. Some of 'em will cut and run. But if anything was to happen to you—"

"They'd all pull out. Is that it?"

"I'm afraid it is, Stu. So see to it nothing happens to you. Hear?"

"Sure, Olaf."

Olaf got up. "I'll sleep in the house until Ernie's caught."

Stuart didn't protest. Olaf went inside, but Stuart remained on the stoop, staring into the darkness. He knew he couldn't sleep yet. He was nervous, and his body ached from the pounding he'd taken at Rifkin's place.

The moon came out from behind a cloud and put a weird, soft light upon the monstrous, wide valley in which Skull lay. By this light, Stuart saw, distantly, a cloud of dust rising from the road. He peered intently, trying to make it out.

It could be an attack on Skull. The lower valley ranchers, having been refused, might have overpowered Skull's three-man guard on the fence . . .

Then he relaxed, stood up and moved ahead. That was a single rider, probably one of the guards.

The rider turned into into the lane. Uneasiness kept growing in Stuart, aroused by the rider's obvious haste. Something had happened, something more than a simple attack on the fence. Besides, if there had been an attack the sound of rifles booming would have carried this far easily in the still, evening air.

Then, as the rider pulled up in the yard, Stuart saw that it was a woman. She swung to the ground and came running toward the house, and he recognized her.

"What's the matter, Katie? What's happened?"

She stopped abruptly. "Stuart?" Her voice was thin with fright.

"Yes. What's the matter?"

"Where have you been?"

"Right here. Why?" She didn't answer immediately, so he said, "We buried Milo tonight."

A sigh of relief escaped her. "Then you've been here all the time? Since you left our place?"

"Of course. I slept until Rifkin came. When he left, we took Milo up on that knoll behind the house."

She didn't speak and he couldn't see her face clearly

135

in the darkness.

"Katie, damn it, something's happened. What is it?"

"Grady Rifkin's dead."

"Dead? How can that be? He just left here. He was all right then."

"He was shot. In the back. He didn't get a mile below your fence. Wally Stamm found him. They think you did it, Stuart. They've sent for the sheriff. You've got to leave! You've got to get away!"

"Get away hell! I didn't kill him."

"Do you think they'll believe that?"

"The whole crew knows I've been right here."

She said patiently, "Stuart, your crew would lie for you. Everybody knows that."

"Why the hell would I kill Rifkin?" But he knew the answer to that even before the question was out of his mouth. He'd taken a beating from Rifkin and his friends, on Rifkin's place. No more than three hours ago, Rifkin had presented him with a phony bill for cattle supposedly killed by Milo. Probably that bill had been on Rifkin's body when he was found. Motive enough for murder, Stuart realized. At least the sheriff and everyone else would think so.

Not only that, but Stuart was tarred with the same brush as Milo and Ernie had been. The whole country knew what Milo would have done to Rifkin for presenting such a phony claim. Milo wouldn't have shot him in the back, but Rifkin wouldn't have left the yard alive.

Everyone knew that Milo had hanged Hugh Shore. They knew Ernie had murdered Milo. It wouldn't be hard for them to believe that Stuart had killed Grady Rifkin.

Stuart said slowly, "I didn't kill him, but someone did. The question is, who?"

"Ernie?"

"No. Ernie's up on top. Or at least I think he is. And anyway, why would Ernie kill Rifkin? He'd have no way of knowing about that phony cattle bill. He sure as hell wouldn't kill Rifkin because he and his friends worked me over. Ernie's done that himself more than once."

"Maybe it was one of Rifkin's friends—one of our neighbors."

"Maybe. But why would they kill him? He was their leader, the strongest one in the bunch."

He could see Katie's face faintly now in the moonlight. She was frowning. And beautiful. In spite of his worry and trouble, he wanted to take her in his arms. Or maybe he wanted to because of his worry and trouble. Katie said, "The quickest, easiest way for them to get Skull would be to get rid of you. Milo's dead and Ernie's on the run. You're the only one left, Stuart."

Stuart nodded. Katie's suggestion made sense. But if they'd killed him, there'd have been an investigation— maybe even some public indignation. This way . . . it was foolproof. The sheriff would blame Stuart for the killing and so would the rest of the county. With Stuart in jail, they'd not only have a free hand to seize what they wanted of Skull, they'd have the tacit approval of everyone in the county for doing so.

He said decisively, "Come on. I'll get a horse and take you home."

"No! It isn't safe for you."

"Then I'll take you to the fence. That's safe enough. I can send one of the crew the rest of the way with you."

"The sheriff—"

"I know Dan. They won't stampede him tonight. He'll come, but it'll be morning before he does."

He kept thinking of Wally Stamm. Wally hated him more virulently, he supposed, than anyone on the creek. Wally's father had sustained a serious injury in the fight today. Wally would want to get even with him for that and for belittling him in front of his own friends before the fight began. Wally already hated him for humiliating him in front of Katie and Nora Dykes.

Wally was the best suspect he could think of for the killing of Grady Rifkin. He fancied himself quite a gunslinger. He wasn't sure of himself and consequently would covet Rifkin's place as leader of the small ranchers.

Stuart walked across to the corral and caught a horse. He saddled up, then led the animal back to the house. He said, "I'd better tell Olaf what's happened."

He left Katie holding both horses and went inside. Olaf was on the couch in the living room where Ernie had slept last night. He wasn't asleep, and raised his head as Stuart came in.

"Katie Dykes is outside," Stuart said. "She rode up to tell me that someone shot Grady Rifkin in the back.

I'm going to take her home."

"Don't go beyond the fence. If they get their hands on you now, you're finished."

Stuart grunted agreement. "Better wake someone and put him on guard. No telling what might happen now."

He went back out, hearing the couch creak behind him. Olaf had been right. He was no better than wild game tonight.

He'd be shot on sight. If he were dead, unable to testify in his own behalf, there'd be no doubt in anyone's mind that he had murdered Rifkin.

He smiled grimly. He had to stay alive.

He helped Katie to mount, then swung to the back of his own horse. They rode out, side by side, and headed downcountry in the thin, cold moonlight.

Stuart felt trapped. Hate was like an epidemic in the country now, a prairie fire sweeping across it from one end to the other. Milo would have stopped it in its tracks. Milo would have taken the crew and burned out every one of the lower valley ranchers.

But Stuart wasn't Milo. He could never be like Milo. He'd fight, but it would always be a defensive fight, never an aggressive, preventive war such as Milo might have waged.

He scowled, aware that Katie was watching his face. He recalled the questions she had asked upon her arrival. She had not been sure of him. Half her terror had been occasioned by her doubt. She thought he might have killed Grady Rifkin.

His scowl faded. He couldn't blame her. Her experience certainly wouldn't tend to make her trust men. Particularly not men named Post.

Her voice was almost a cry. "Stuart, I'm frightened. What's going to happen? What are you going to do? Nobody will believe that you never left the house tonight. Nobody else had a reason for wanting Grady Rifkin dead."

He knew she needed reassurance. He said, "Don't worry. Everything will be all right." But he wasn't sure of that himself. He was beginning to wonder how it could. Tomorrow the sheriff would be up with a posse. Stuart would be faced with a choice—either fight off the sheriff and his posse and make himself an outlaw forever, or submit to arrest and spend several months in jail while Stamm and the others seized what they wanted of Skull and destroyed the rest.

The alternatives were intolerable. Yet he could see no other choice.

The miles between the house and the fence dwindled. Stuart began to feel uneasy, and was relieved when the moon slipped behind a cloud. It wouldn't be too hard for one of Skull's enemies to slip through the fence in the darkness. Three men couldn't guard the whole length of it from rim to rim. Even now someone might be hiding on the hillside, watching the road. The man who had shot Rifkin in the back wouldn't hesitate to kill Stuart the same way.

He wished Katie and Nora were still in town. He wished he could be sure that they would be safe in the days to come.

Katie rode in silence beside him. At ten, they

approached the fence and were challenged by the guard.

Despite Katie's protests, Stuart rode on through with her. If someone was waiting to ambush him below the fence, he didn't want to send one of the crewmen into the ambush. Nor did he want Katie riding into it alone. Someone in this valley was trigger-happy enough to shoot first and ask questions later. In darkness, Katie could be mistaken for a man.

But the distance between the fence and Nora's house dropped behind without incident. And at ten-fifteen, they rode into sight of Nora's yard.

CHAPTER FIFTEEN

The house was dark. Katie drew rein as soon as she sighted it. Stuart halted beside her.

Her voice was soft, almost a whisper. "Don't ride in with me. Someone might be waiting, someone who saw me ride toward Skull."

Stuart dismounted, expecting her to go on. Instead she stepped down too, dropping the reins of her horse. She stood there hesitantly in the darkness, and then came toward him.

He held out his arms and she ran to them, trembling a little, but eager too.

He felt a vast, protective compassion. So many things were troubling Katie. Fear for his safety, fear of the future. She was afraid of love, but she needed it too.

He held her very close until her trembling stopped.

Then he tipped up her face and kissed her on the mouth. Her response was slow to come, but when it did, it was almost frantic. Her body pressed warmly against him and her mouth clung to his avidly.

He whispered, "Katie, Katie, we should have gone away."

"Yes. But you'd have had to come back."

"I know." He wondered if the time would come when peace would again reign in this valley. He wondered if he would be alive and free to enjoy it.

And he knew a sudden, almost panicky fear for Katie's safety. She and her mother were right in the middle, involved whether they wanted to be or not. Wally Stamm would be itching to prove himself with them. Ernie would be wild with hatred for Nora. Sooner or later, Ernie would return for his revenge. And Stuart could not even offer protection to them. His own fate was in doubt. The sheriff would be up here after him with a posse tomorrow.

He kissed Katie again, wishing he could just carry her back to Skull with him. If he didn't send her in now, he never would.

He said, "Go on in, Katie. Go on, or I'll never let you go."

"No. I want to stay with you." He heard a branch crack nearby, and stiffened. His hands tightened on Katie's arms. His voice was barely audible. "Someone's there."

Katie's horse had wandered toward the clearing, its reins trailing. Katie began to shiver again. Listening intently, Stuart heard what sounded like a boot scuffed in dry dirt from the other direction.

God! They were all around him. And the minute Katie tried to go in . . . they'd cut her down, believing her to be Stuart. It wasn't light enough to tell a woman from a man. "Call out to your mother," he whispered. "Then walk slowly toward the cabin. Don't move fast and don't try to move without being seen."

He was glad, now, that he'd brought Katie all the way home. If he hadn't, she might have stopped a bullet before they realized who she was. Katie clung to him. He disengaged her hands firmly. "Go on! Now!"

She moved hesitantly away. His heart sank. Katie's fright was making her move almost stealthily in spite of herself. He seized the reins of his horse. He whispered urgently, "Call out to your mother!"

She called "Mother!" but her voice broke on the last syllable.

A gun flared, its lance-like flame pointing directly at Katie. She started violently, and then began to run.

Stuart bellowed, "You dumb son-of-a bitch! You're shooting at Katie! I'm over here!"

He vaulted to the back of his horse. Two more guns opened up, one from the back wall of Nora's house, one from the direction of that telltale scuffing boot.

He reined his plunging horse around. He spurred savagely, not up the lane toward the road, but straight into the high brush.

Dodging, twisting, his horse lunged frantically away, as startled by the sudden shots as Stuart was. Almost immediately he heard horses thundering in pursuit.

143

Bullets probed the brush for him, but at least no more were fired back there at the house.

Wally Stamm's shrill, ragged voice shouted, "This way! He went this way!"

"Somebody take the road!" Tim Boorom bawled. "Cut him off!"

Anticipating that, Stuart had already swung toward the road. Fighting through the brush was too damned slow. It gave him protection from their probing bullets, but that wouldn't help him much if he allowed one of them to get ahead of him.

Anger born of helplessness, persecution, injustice, rankled in Stuart. It was all he could do to keep from stopping, from shooting it out with them.

He restrained himself with difficulty. He was in enough trouble now, without making it worse. Innocent of Rifkin's murder he might, with luck, get out of that. If he killed one of these others here tonight, he'd be finished.

He reached the road, swung into it, his horse skidding as he turned. He thundered toward the fence, raking the horse cruelly with his spurs.

He heard them turn into the road behind him, heard their rifles open up. He glanced at the sky. The moon, slipping from behind a cloud, would bathe the road with light in another couple of minutes.

Stuart leaned low against his horse's withers. A bullet tore into the hard-packed road beside him, ricocheted and whined away upcountry.

Ahead lay the fence. Just a half mile away.

Up in the cedars, on both sides of the creek, a man

was stationed. Another at the gate. The moon slipped from behind the cloud almost reluctantly.

Stuart made a target now. A quarter mile . . ."

A gun up in the cedars flared. Again. From the other side, the gun of the second guard barked. The sounds rolled up against the towering rims and echoed back, again and again.

Those behind him were shooting almost frantically now. Stuart swung his head. They were all there. Tim Doorem and his brother Juko. Vince Doyle. Wally Stamm. At least four, anyway.

Four against him tonight. Tomorrow the odds would change. The sheriff would have ten men or more.

The gate was open, and as Stuart thundered through, the guard opened fire.

Stuart hauled up. He turned his horse and rode back to the gate. The four had stopped and taken cover in the brush beside the road. They were shooting now at the flashes up in the hills, at the flashes of the guard's gun here at the gate.

"That's enough," Stuart said. "You won't hit any-thing."

The guard on the gate was Ken Ivy. "Let's go get 'em."

"That would just about prove I killed Rifkin. No, Ken. Let 'em go."

He turned his horse. Katie was safe for now. He'd pulled them away from her. He said bruskly, "Stay awake," and rode toward home.

As far as he could see, things were fast going from bad to worse. The law wanted him for murder, and tomorrow he would have to make a choice between surrendering or fighting.

If he chose to fight, he would find every hand in the country against him. As an outlaw, he could count on only a few days before his crew deserted and a posse took him. Or, if he chose to flee, he would leave behind everything that mattered to him.

Not much of a choice. No choice at all.

Scowling thoughtfully, he rode along until he was well clear of the fence. The crew couldn't be expected to lay their lives on the line for a lost cause. It wasn't right to ask it of them. In fighting for Stuart, they would only make outlaws of themselves. And if anyone was killed in the ruckus . . .

Suddenly, decisively, he reined up. Slanting away from the road, he climbed his horse steadily through the cedars for twenty minutes. He climbed the shaly, talus slope below the rim, and when he reached it, three quarters of an hour after leaving the road, he headed east toward town.

He rode carefully on the narrow shelf below the rim. It was slow going, but he had all night.

At the fence, he dismounted and silently took down the wires. He led his horse through, keeping a watchful eye on the place the guard was stationed.

Once through, he replaced the fence. He wouldn't be coming back this way. Maybe he wouldn't be coming back at all.

Looking down into the wide, moon-washed valley, he checked Nora's house, a thousand feet below. It was dark, as was Rifkin's, a mile farther on. He saw light in

Stamm's place, but none in either Doyle's or Boorom's. Stuart guessed they had gathered at Stamm's to plan their next move.

Somebody was scared down there, or that ambush attempt would never have been made. All they'd had to do was wait until morning and let the sheriff and his posse take Stuart. The ambush had been chancy and dangerous. Somebody wanted him dead before the sheriff reached him.

He wondered if they would try to attack Skull yet tonight. He doubted it. There were only four of them, not enough to mount a successful attack on Skull. No. They probably would wait until morning now, and join the sheriff's posse as it rode toward Skull.

Doing so would put them inside its boundaries, in a position to fire that "accidental" shot that would cut him down before he had a chance to surrender.

Slowly, the lower valley places fell behind. Midnight passed, and one o'clock. The moon dropped steadily toward the western horizon.

He dropped down into the valley more than a mile above town, and rode watchfully along the road, ready to run if he should meet anyone traveling it.

He met no one. The road was deserted.

Peering down into the town from a high place in the road half a mile above it, he saw that it was almost completely dark. Only the hotel and one of the saloons showed light.

He left the main road at the edge of town and entered by a back street in the residential section. His horse's hoofs made little noise on the dusty street. Saddle leather creaked occasionally. Otherwise all was still.

A cat yowled on a back fence, and a dog began to bark. In a stable, somewhere, a horse whinnied.

This was the dangerous part. If one person spotted him the whole town would be out hunting in a matter of minutes. He would be harried like a rabbit with a pack of dogs at his heels.

He knew of two places where he should find the sheriff. One was the jail, where he always slept when he had a prisoner locked up. The other was the hotel, where he slept when the jail was empty. Since he had no way of knowing whether the jail was empty or not, he had no alternative but to check both places.

Checking the jail would be easy. It sat at the end of First Street next to the barbershop and far enough from the saloon so that it took a considerable commotion at the jail to be heard at the saloon.

The hotel, however, offered a real problem. A sleepy clerk was on duty in the lobby all night. He napped occasionally, but it was all but impossible to enter the lobby without wakening him. Dan Mountain's room was on the second floor front, down the long main hall from the head of the stairs. From experience, Stuart knew that both the stairs and the hallway floor squeaked noisily. And there were no back stairs.

So he hoped fervently that he'd find Mountain sleeping at the jail.

He circled his horse through the silent, sleeping town, judging the time at somewhere between two and two-thirty. This time of year it got light damned early. The eastern sky would be fairly gray by three.

He came up on the jail from its far side, dismounted beside it and tied his horse securely. Walking, he rounded the corner of the sun sandstone building, his bootheels sounding hollowly on the boardwalk.

He halted by the front door and listened. He heard no sound. He tried the door. It was locked.

That didn't mean anything. Dan Mountain always locked it at night, even when he was sleeping here. But there was one way to tell for sure.

Fumbling upward in the darkness, Stuart's hand encountered a padlock and hasp. Locked from the outside. That meant the jail was empty.

Bleak discouragement bore down on Stuart Post. Luck had certainly deserted him. Now he had to take the greater risk and find Dan at the hotel.

He went back to his horse and untied the reins. Leading the animal, he walked up the center of the dusty street. Dogs were less likely to bark at him if he moved openly. And it wasn't likely he'd meet anyone.

He passed the saloon, momentarily holding his breath. Through the dirty, fly-specked windows of the place, he could see Josh Dunham, the town drunk, sleeping with his head on the bar. There was another man at the bar, whom Stuart didn't recognize, and Tap Cates, the bartender, standing behind it.

Then he was clear, and heading toward the corner of First and Main, where the hotel stood.

He could feel his nerves draw tight. He could feel a touch of fear. Once he went into the hotel and up those stairs, he'd be trapped. If someone saw him and gave the alarm, even a sleepy hotel resident rising early . . ."

He put nervousness from him determinedly. He had only one chance of getting clear and this was it.

He'd go through with it and if the town treed him in the hotel, by God they'd know they'd been in a fight.

CHAPTER SIXTEEN

Stuart halted before the three-story hotel and stared warily up and down the street. There was some risk involved in tying his horse here. Being the only one at the rail, it was bound to attract attention. If someone happened to investigate, and saw the Skull brand on the horse's hip . . .

Almost angrily he looped the horse's reins and climbed the steps to the lobby door. Chances were slim that anyone would be up and around before three. And by then he would be gone.

He pulled open the lobby door. It squeaked loudly. He slipped inside and stood silently with his back to it, his eyes on the clerk, his hand on his gun.

The clerk sat in a swivel chair before a roll-top desk behind the curving counter. Stuart could see his head, tipped aside against the chair back, and his feet, keeping the register company up on the desk. The man was snoring softly.

Stuart crossed the lobby, walking carefully on its toes.

He passed the desk ten feet away. The sleeping clerk grunted, and shifted, but did not awaken. Just a little more, and Stuart would be on the stairs.

He reached them, looking over his shoulder watchfully at the clerk. Maybe he'd be smarter to go back and slug the man. But he didn't want to. Men sometimes died from blows on the head and a nervous hand is likely to strike too hard.

He stepped up and began to climb the stairs. On the fifth stair, the boards underfoot creaked thunderously.

The clerk's swivel chair creaked too as he sat up. Stuart bounded for the top of the stairs.

He reached them. Now only his boots were visible to the clerk. He slowed and walked, in what he judged was a sleepy, reluctant manner, down the musty-smelling, dimly lighted hall.

He hoped the clerk would be too sleepy to pay much attention, that he'd assume Stuart was simply a late returning resident at the hotel. Apparently he did, for there was no outcry from the lobby.

Down the hall Stuart went, pausing at the sheriff's door. He had no way of knowing whether the sheriff habitually locked his door at night or not. He could only hope he didn't.

He tried the knob and it turned easily. The door opened, squeaking faintly. Stuart stepped inside.

Dan Mountain was a lumped shape on the bed over beside the window. The feeble shaft of gray light from the eastern sky illuminated his sleeping form.

Stuart drew his gun and crossed the room. He thumbed back the hammer, sat down on the side of the bed. He rammed the gun into the sheriff's back, at the same time putting his hand over the sheriff's mouth.

Dan woke convulsively and tried to turn. Stuart didn't try to hold him. He just dug the gun harder into the sheriff's body and said, "Take it easy, Dan, or you're dead. Turn slow and don't try to reach your gun."

Dan Mountain froze. "That's better," Stuart said. "Now we can talk."

"It's Stuart, isn't it?"

"Yes."

"What the hell do *you* want?"

"You."

"Me? Why me?"

"If you're not in town in the morning you can't very well organize a posse, now can you?"

"You're too late, Stu. The posse is already organized. All we're waiting for is daylight. Better give up and save trouble all the way around."

"Uh-uh. I didn't kill Rifkin."

"If you didn't, the jury will set you free."

"You're talking like a fool, Dan. You know as well as I do what would happen if I ever came to trial. They wouldn't be trying me. They'd be trying Skull—trying Milo and Ernie for all the things that have happened in the last twenty years."

Stuart got up and backed away from the bed. "Put on your clothes. You're coming with me."

"Where? What for?"

"Maybe we'll try and find out who really killed Rifkin. I think we can start with Wally Stamm."

"To hell with you. I'm not coming."

"Quit wasting your breath, Dan. You're going with me. Whether you do it with a lump on your head or without is up to you."

He meant exactly what he said. He had gone too far to back out now.

Dan must have believed he would too, for he swung his feet over the side of the bed and reached for his pants. Stuart said, "Don't pull anything, Dan. Don't try being a hero. Look at it this way. Your job is to find Rifkin's killer. I want that as much as you do."

Dan didn't speak. But neither did he reach for his gun and belt.

Stuart stepped across to the foot of the bed where it hung from the brass bedpost. He removed the gun and stuck it into his belt. The he handed Dan the belt. Dan strapped it on. Stuart said, "After you, sheriff."

Dan whirled on him. "Damn it, Stu, you're only making things tougher for yourself."

"They can be worse?"

Dan grunted. He opened the door and stepped into the hall. Stuart stopped him at the head of the stairs. He removed the cartridges from Dan's gun and returned the weapon to him. He put his own gun into his belt and buttoned his coat over it. He whispered, "I've surrendered to you, Dan. That's what you tell the clerk if he asks. You're taking me to jail. But don't drop behind me. Don't risk that clerk's life and your own. You're not even sure I killed Rifkin, and until you are . . ." He left the sentence dangling.

Dan started down the stairs, with Stuart keeping pace. Abreast, they reached the foot of the stairs.

The clerk, awake now, looked up. "I thought I saw someone—"

Dan said, "He surrendered himself, Si. It's all right."

Si started around the corner of the counter. "Good thing he did, too. Shootin' a man in the back!"

"Never mind, Si," the sheriff said sharply. "Never mind. He's not convicted yet."

"No, and maybe he won't even go to trial. People are pretty sore . . ."

They reached the door with the clerk trailing twenty feet behind. For appearances sake, Stuart went out first, warily, his head turned to watch Dan. The sheriff might have tried slugging him as he went through the door. With Stuart watching him, he didn't get the chance.

Out on the walk in the deep gray light of dawn, Stuart asked, "Where's the quickest place to get a horse?"

Dan Mountain hesitated.

"We can ride double," Stuart said harshly. "Take your choice."

"I've got one stabled behind the jail."

"All right. Get going."

He untied the reins of his horse and mounted. As he rode away following Dan he glanced at the hotel doorway. The clerk, Si Dean, was standing there. In the poor light, Stuart couldn't see Dean's face. He wished he could. Then he'd know if his words to Dan had been overheard.

Dan strode away down the street and turned the corner. The lamps were dark, now, inside the saloon. No horses were tied in front. But Tap Cates was just coming out, locking the door behind him.

Stuart held his breath, his mind racing. Frantically,

he tried to think of something that would keep Cates from getting curious.

Cates turned and peered through the strengthening light at the pair. Maybe, thought Stuart, it was still too dark for recognition. He whispered urgently, "Tell him you're getting the posse ready to go. Tell him to get his horse and come along."

Dan trudged ahead of him, stubbornly silent. Stuart snarled, "Tell him, damn you, or I'll ride you down!"

Dan stopped and glared furiously up at him. He turned to look at Cates. He called, "Posse's almost ready to go, Tap. Come on if you're coming."

Tap stepped to the edge of the walk. He said sourly, "Not me, sheriff. I'm going home to bed. I've been up all night."

"Suit yourself," Dan replied, and Tap turned to tramp along the walk toward home.

Stuart released a long, slow sigh of relief. The town would know soon enough that Dan was gone. But by that time Stuart hoped to be ten or fifteen miles away.

CHAPTER SEVENTEEN

Stuart and the sheriff made it almost to the edge of town. The sky was lighter gray now, and spread enough cold light in the street to see all the way across it.

A door slamming made Stuart look apprehensively at one of the houses they were approaching. A man had come out on the porch. He peered curiously at the two riders.

155

Recognizing the sheriff, he called, "Heading out already, Dan? I thought you wanted a posse."

The sheriff hesitated. "Answer him!" Stuart whispered. savagely.

Dan Mountain called, "I do want a posse, Frank. Tell 'em to head out as quick as they can get mounted. This here's Stuart Post and he's got a gun in my back."

Stuart jabbed his spurs into his startled horse's sides. As he drew abreast of Dan's mount, he cut the animal across the rump with the barrel of his gun. The horse bounded ahead into a hard run.

Stuart stayed half a length behind, yelling now at the frantic horse Dan rode, "Hi-yah! Yah! Get out of here!"

Together they thundered out of town, taking the road leading up the valley through the high sagebrush and greasewood. Above them loomed the brooding rims, gray and somehow menacing in the pre-dawn light.

Stuart knew he had cut off a big bite. There'd be a dozen men pounding after him in fifteen or twenty minutes. Even if he managed to maintain that lead, it wouldn't give him much time for sweating the truth out of Wally Stamm. Unless Dan Mountain would cooperate.

He surged up beside Dan's horse. "You couldn't have been very scared of me or you wouldn't have done that. Hell, you know I didn't kill Grady."

"The hell I do. I just knew you wouldn't shoot me down in front of a witness."

"You still think I'd shoot a man in the back?"

Reluctant doubt seemed to be bothering Dan Mountain. After a moment he replied, "Maybe you did that just to throw me off. How do I know?"

"I'm not that sly. Damn it Dan, be fair."

"Fair? God almighty! You come to my room in the middle of the night and ram a gun in my back. You make me look like a jackass in front of the whole town by kidnapping me the day I'm supposed to go after you. And then you ask me to be fair! To hell with you!"

Stuart kept his mouth shut. They rode another half mile and at last Dan Mountain asked grumpily, "What do you want?"

"I want to tackle Wally Stamm. He's the only one who could have killed Grady and I think he's yellow as hell. Put a little pressure on him and he'll crack wide open."

Dan studied his face. At last he nodded sourly. "I don't know what the hell I've got to say about it anyhow."

Faint blue came to the sky. The high, thin clouds turned pink. The sun poked up over the rims, staining the crags to westward a brilliant orange. After riding another mile, Stuart yelled, "When are you going after Ernie?"

Dan glared at him. "Whenever you get through playing games. That's what the posse was for, until Tim Boorom rode in last night to tell me about Grady. I was going to pick you up this morning and send you back with a couple of men while I got on Ernie's trail. Goddam it, I wish I'd never heard of the Post family!"

Stuart frowned. He hoped desperately that he'd guessed right about Wally killing Rifkin. The sheriff was getting more soreheaded by the minute. Later, he'd be worse, because he'd be getting hungry and would miss his morning coffee.

Wally seemed like the only logical suspect, but Stuart knew he couldn't be entirely sure. Ernie might have done it. Any of the lower valley ranchers might have done it. He had no guarantee that his guess about Wally was right.

And if it wasn't . . . Well, his time would have run out. The posse would catch up. He'd be taken into custody and thrown in jail to rot. Skull would be fair prey for every hungry cowman whose land bordered on it. By the time he got out of jail, if he ever did, Skull would be only a memory, only a few deeded sections of hayland and a house.

He sorted out the lower valley ranchers in his mind apprehensively. Tim Boorom, squat and thick, was certainly capable of killing, but Stuart doubted if he'd do it just to throw suspicion on another man. Kill he might, for personal reasons or in anger. But not this way.

Boorom's brother Jake was an older copy of Tim, only more shiftless and untidy. He rarely shaved and his straggly whiskers were perpetually stained with chewing tobacco. Stuart shook his head. Not Jake. He was sure of that.

Vince Doyle was a cut above the others. Tall, soldierly, dignified, he never seemed quite comfortable in range clothes. Doyle was a retired army sergeant who had held brevet rank during the war. Stuart couldn't imagine Doyle ever shooting anyone in the back, though he sure as hell had taken part in beating Stuart yesterday. Still, when a man's back is to the wall he does a lot of things he wouldn't ordinarily do. Yesterday's beating had been the result of hysteria and accumulated anger. Last night's killing had been coldly premeditated. Stuart shook his head imperceptibly. It couldn't have been Vince Doyle.

Which left only Wally and his father, Nick. And Nick was crippled from that pitchfork wound. He always came back to Wally Stamm. Wally was sly, in a crazy sort of way. He fancied himself a gunfighter. He would be anxious to establish himself head of the valley ranchers if possible.

They passed Boorom's place, and Doyle's. And at last came in sight of Stamm's small bachelor spread.

Water had been spread over the fields at both Boorom's and Doyle's. There was none out on the fields at Stamm's.

Wally didn't want to work at ranching, Stuart realized, and suddenly felt more sure of himself. If Wally hadn't had some other plan, he would have overcome his reluctance, and spread some of that water out over his hay.

The house was frame, and once had been painted white. All the paint had weathered away, leaving the boards warped, the house a dingy gray. Holes in the shingle roof had been patched with tin. Now the tin was rusty and showed red against the shingles' gray.

The creek ran behind the house. Between the house and road the brush grew high, so Stuart chose that route of approach.

Remembering the incident in town, Stuart drew his

gun. He said, "Stay ahead of me Dan. And don't try to bolt. Maybe I won't shoot you, but I'll shoot your horse."

"How the hell do you think you're goin' to make him talk?" Mountain asked surlily.

"I'll let him know you're a prisoner and can't interfere. I'll tell him it's talk or get strung up like Hugh Shore. That'll put the fear of God into him."

"I just hope you're right."

"I'm right. I know it wasn't me, even if you don't. So who else could it have been but Wally?"

They rode in, Dan with his hands on the saddle horn, Stuart holding his gun pointed loosely at Dan's back. Not even a chicken scratched in the deep, dry dust. Stuart saw one horse in the corral, and a saddle on the ground beside the gate.

Nervousness tightened his throat. Wally was dangerous. Kill-crazy dangerous. What if he didn't wait for talk? What if he just cut down on them from ambush?

But he couldn't play this safe. There simply wasn't time. He followed the sheriff to the center of the yard, moved slightly past him and bellowed, "Wally! Nick!"

He saw the windowshade in one of the windows stir and an instant later saw the revolver barrel that poked through a tear in it. He started to swing his gun, opened his mouth to yell at Dan.

Before he could do either, the gun in the window spit smoke and flame.

He winced involuntarily in expectation of the bullet's impact. When it didn't strike, a faint tingle of surprise and relief ran through him. Wally ought to be able to shoot better than that.

His own gun bucked in his hand, a fraction of a second after he heard Wally's bullet strike. He swung his head toward Dan, just in time to see the sheriff topple from his saddle. Dan struck the ground wholly limp and lay still afterward in a peculiarly twisted position. A shock of horror numbed Stuart's mind. Good God! Had the whole country gone completely mad?

Wally's revolver roared again as Stuart swung back. This time the bullet must have ticked Stuart's horse. The animal gave a shrill snort and reared. He began to buck furiously, straight toward the wall of the house.

Stuart left him fifteen feet from the house. He hit the ground running, lost his footing and rolled until he banged up against the wall. The horse kept going and disappeared around the corner. While Stuart lay there, breathing hoarsely, the sheriff's horse trotted after it.

Gray, hopeless discouragement touched him. This had turned into a waking nightmare. He hadn't surprised Wally; the locoed little gunny had surprised him. He just hadn't figured Wally would shoot at the sheriff first. And he'd been willing to take the chance of being shot himself.

The way things stood now, Stuart couldn't win. He had kidnapped the sheriff at gunpoint earlier this morning. Nobody would believe Wally had killed the sheriff. They already believed Stuart had shot Rifkin in the back.

He cursed, softly, savagely, lying there against the

weather-beaten wall of Stamm's house, he began to get mad, so mad that he forgot fear.

Blood raced through his body. Recklessness possessed him. No longer was there anything for him to lose. Get him they might, but not before he got Wally Stamm, and not without a fight. Nor would they get him alive. They weren't going to pen him up to rot.

He eased slowly to his feet, staying close to the wall, keeping his eyes warily on the window.

He called, "Wally? You'd better come out, you son-of-a-bitch, or I'm coming in after you."

No answer. Stuart roared, "Wally!"

Then it came—a high-pitched screech of demented defiance.

"Come on, Post. Come on, damn you! I'll cut you down as you come through the door!"

Stuart stepped slightly away from the wall. The Stamm shack wasn't very big and only had one door. Wally had fired and yelled from the bedroom window. Besides the bedroom, there was only the kitchen. If he could circle all the way around the house and reach the door . . . or if he could make Wally think that was what he intended to do . . .

The silence in the yard was complete. Only the murmur of the creek intruded. Stuart slipped around the corner of the house.

Wally yelled, "You're licked damn you! All I got to do is sit tight. If you kidnapped the sheriff, there's sure as hell a posse somewhere close behind. Besides, I watched you comin' up the creek. You wouldn't have been ridin' that way unless someone was on your tail."

Stuart didn't answer. If he just kept still, he'd get Wally to worrying about where he was and what he was doing. Wally's nerves weren't good anyway. Like many gunmen, he killed out of a sort of tormented hysteria. If he got worried enough, he might panic and make some crazy bad move.

Through the thin back wall, he heard Wally's steps inside the house. He crept along the wall. As he ducked under the kitchen window, he heard Wally yell, "I can see the door and both windows now. By God, we'll see if you can wait as long as I can!"

Silence stretched out painfully. Stuart knew he had been here nearly ten minutes. That gave him only ten more before the posse would arrive. Wally *could* outwait him. Wally had all the time in the world.

Stuart had to make his play. Still creeping along, he shouted, "You can't watch two windows and a door at the same time. You don't know which one I'll show up in. Better come out, Wally. Maybe the sheriff isn't dead."

No answer. Stuart yelled, "What'd you shoot him for anyway? Why not me?"

He kept moving, hearing Wally's reply, muffled by the wall of the house. "Why should I shoot you? Hell, the posse will take care of you. They won't believe I killed the sheriff, they'll think you did. I doubt if you'll even get to town alive."

Stuart reached the side of the door and stopped. Wally's voice, clearer now, went on. "They already think you shot Rifkin in the back. It won't be hard for 'em to believe you killed the sheriff too."

"You killed Rifkin, didn't you, Wally?"

No answer. And Stuart had given away his position.

He yelled, "I'm leaving, Wally. I'm going up where Rifkin's body was found and look for tracks."

He heard Wally's steps crossing the room. He stepped away from the door. He'd know in a minute what Wally was going to do. He'd either come out this door, or he'd cover Stuart's horse from the kitchen window.

Wally apparently chose the window, for his next shout came from there. "You can save yourself the time. Sure I killed Rifkin—shot him in the back so you wouldn't be able to claim it was a fight. Go ahead. Try to reach your horse!"

Stuart stepped to the door and kicked it open. He leaped inside and out of the doorway.

It was nearly dark inside with all the shades drawn. After the brilliance of the sunlight outside, Stuart couldn't see very well. But he did catch a blur of movement over against the kitchen window.

Then, in the bedroom, Nick Stamm groaned. Bed springs creaked as he tried to get up, and in the same instant, flame lanced from the window toward Stuart.

The bullet tore a chunk of the door jamb away close beside him. He fired instinctively at the flash, and then he crossed the room at a run, not particularly caring whether Wally hit him or not. Just so he got to Wally first.

CHAPTER EIGHTEEN

Wally shot once more, and this bullet burned through the fleshy part of Stuart's upper arm. But he could see Wally now, and his gun centered exactly on Wally's chest before he released the hammer.

The gun bellowed, and a cloud of powdersmoke rolled out. Wally slammed back against the flimsy wall, shaking it, causing cans to cascade from a shelf.

Stuart didn't stop to examine Wally's body. He knew where his bullet had struck. Instead he turned and bolted for the door. In a moment, Nick Stamm would be on his feet, reaching for a gun.

Stuart ran outside. He crossed the yard and knelt at the sheriff's side.

Dan was conscious. His eyes blinked against the direct sunlight. Stuart shaded his face with his hat and asked urgently, "Where are you hit, Dan?"

"Chest. Get me some help, Stu."

"Sure, Dan. Sure I will." He hesitated, glanced at the house and back at Dan. Town was too far. Dan wouldn't make it, bleeding this way. There was no decent care for him here.

Nora could care for him though—clean his wound and put him into bed. He said, "I've got to load you on a horse. It'll hurt, Dan."

"Nora's?"

"It's the only place. It's only a couple of miles."

"Go ahead."

Stuart stooped. As he slid his arms under the sheriff's

body, Dan whispered, "I heard the son-of-a-bitch. You're clear with me, Stu."

Stuart grinned with relief. "Then don't die until you tell someone."

He lifted the sheriff and staggered toward his horse. Dan was heavy and he had to be handled with care.

Nick Stamm had found a rifle somewhere. He opened up on them from the kitchen window. Stuart laid Dan's body over his horse. Without tying him down, he led the horse away into the brush.

His own horse followed, fortunately. And also fortunately, Nick Stamm's wound was too painful for him to shoot accurately. He missed cleanly with all of the four or five shots he fired.

Dan Mountain was unconscious. Stuart tore a piece out of the back of his shirt and wadded it against the wound in Dan's chest. Then he tied Dan down, picked up the reins of the sheriff's horse and mounted his own.

Even the movement of a slowly traveling horse would keep Dan's wound bleeding. A fast traveling horse would make it no worse. And time might save Dan's life.

Besides, Stuart knew what would happen if the posse caught him now. Nick Stamm would swear he had killed both the sheriff and Wally. The posse wouldn't give him time to explain anything. They'd shoot on sight.

He rode out through the brush to the road. Down toward town he could see a rising cloud of dust. The posse. They'd stop at Stamm's, probably, having heard the shots. They'd take a few minutes there. Maybe enough time for Stuart to reach Nora's ahead of them.

When he reached the road, he spurred his horse to a gallop, watching over his shoulder to see that Dan didn't slip. It seemed to be an easy gait for Dan's inert body, which moved even less galloping than it did at a trot. And the motion was smoother.

He wished he knew how bad the sheriff's wound was. A chest wound was always serious, but not always fatal. It depended on what it hit as it passed on through—lungs, arteries—sometimes on how close it came to the heart. Maybe Dan wouldn't even reach Nora's place alive. If he didn't, Stuart was in much worse trouble than before.

He passed Rifkin's place, riding hard. His own flesh wound was bleeding freely, but he knew it wasn't serious, even though loss of blood might weaken him. With luck, this would soon be over. If Dan regained consciousness long enough to tell that posse what he knew . . .

Wally was dead, and so was Rifkin. There'd be no more trouble out of the lower valley bunch.

He could see Nora out in the brush behind the house trying to catch a horse as he rode in. She was running, and obviously nearly hysterical. The waving of her skirts and her hysteria only further frightened the horse she was trying to catch. He ran in circles around her, keeping well clear of her.

She saw Stuart and began to run toward the house. She fell twice. She splashed across the creek in water to her knees, making no attempt to keep her skirts clear.

Stuart dismounted, untied Dan and slid him out of the saddle. He could hear Nora screaming at him but he didn't stop.

Something within him told him what had happened. His chest felt as though it were filled with ice. Ernie had come back. Nursing hate like a wounded bear, he had come back to get his revenge.

Not physically against Nora. No. That would be too easy. Ernie had taken Katie, probably after telling Nora, in detail, what he meant to do to her.

Stuart wanted to drop the sheriff and run outside. He could hear some of Nora's words now, and knew his guess had been correct. She kept screaming, "Katie! Katie! He's got her!"

Stuart carried the sheriff to the bed and laid him down gently. Nora burst in the door, completely hysterical, completely out of control. She clawed at him and screamed at him.

He slapped her. She shut up then, staring at him with shocked, wondering eyes.

"I know," Stuart said harshly. "Katie's gone. Ernie's got her."

She nodded dumbly.

He tried to sound sure, convincing. "I'll get her back, Nora. Don't worry. Now listen to me."

She nodded again, her stricken eyes clinging to his.

"Dan's been shot, Nora. He's unconscious. You've got to take care of him and see he doesn't die. Get started while I talk."

She hurried to the water bucket standing by the sink. Taking the bucket and some towels which she snatched hastily from a drawer, she went into the bedroom. Stuart followed.

"There's a posse after me. They think I shot Rifkin and Dan and Wally Stamm. They won't bother to ask questions if they catch me. They'll shoot me down and I'll never find Katie."

She was busy with Dan, and her voice was low. "What do you want me to do?"

"Bring him around if you can. He heard Wally admit killing Rifkin. He knows Wally shot him, and can tell the posse if he's conscious. If you can't bring him around, hold the posse here as long as possible. If Dan comes to and tells his story, then send them along after me."

"Where will he take her?"

"Up on top first. After that I don't know. It'll be slow, but I'll just have to trail them."

She looked up. "All right, Stuart. I'm all right now."

"Good. Think Dan will make it?"

"He's lost a lot of blood. I don't know. I'll just do the best I can."

"Try and bring him around."

"Yes, Stuart."

He left her and ran outside. He swung to the saddle, bent down and snatched the reins of Dan Mountain's horse. Then he galloped out of the yard.

He knew that he should have done this yesterday, immediately after he'd found Milo's body. If he had . . .

He caught himself remembering Ernie—the way he

had looked as Hugh Shore's body dangled in the air—the countless other times Ernie had perpetrated some deliberate cruelty.

He thought of Katie in Ernie's hands. He couldn't stop the shudder that traveled down his spine.

There was no time for circling after sign. There was no need for it either. Ernie would not have gone toward town. Nor would he have gone to Skull. That left him but one way out of the valley, the same way he had come in—by trail to the top of the plateau.

Stuart left the road immediately above Nora's house. Thick oakbrush and serviceberry grew here on the hillside, screening him from the road below. After a few minutes, he climbed out of the brush and entered the cedars.

Climbing steadily, he reached the foot of the talus slide fifteen minutes after leaving the road. He swung around in the saddle, without stopping, and scanned the valley below.

Nora's yard was full of saddle horses. He could see several men standing around.

Dan Mountain's posse. He wondered if Dan would ever regain consciousness. He wondered if he'd regain it in time to change the posse's purpose from that of killing or capturing Stuart to helping him catch Ernie.

He shrugged fatalistically. Whatever the posse did, they'd not keep him from Ernie. He had a lead on them now—fifteen minutes at the least. How much more lead he gained depended pretty much on Nora.

But he knew the top of the plateau better than any man in the posse. They wouldn't catch him there.

All his life he had fought Ernie. Never had he beaten him. But neither had he knuckled under. Always the fighting had been with fists. The only time Stuart had threatened Ernie with a gun was the day he and Milo had hanged Hugh Shore.

Then, he'd found himself unable to use it. He'd still supposed that Ernie was his brother. Now he knew otherwise. He knew exactly what Ernie was.

This time, the fight would be with guns, and to the death. Only one of them would leave the plateau alive.

He crossed the steep slide, keeping his horse at a fast walk, still trailing the sheriff's horse behind. By switching mounts when one or the other played out, he'd be able to travel farther and faster.

At the foot of the rim, he found the trail of Ernie's horse, and another—coming down—these tracks overlaid with fresher ones, going up.

He touched his horse's sides with his spurs. The animal lunged upward over the narrow shelf trail.

Apprehensively, Stuart stared upward. Here would be a good place for Ernie to get him or drive him back. Stuart was completely exposed, and would be until he reached the top. Ernie, on the other hand, could lie up there concealed and fire at will. Or roll rocks down across the trail.

Up, up he went, his horse scrambling at times on the narrow, rock-strewn trail. He reached the halfway point, and his nervousness increased. Ahead lay the worst stretch, one into which channeled a small ravine or cut in the rim that led straight out to the top. A rock rolled down that ravine would gather more as it came,

171

until it had started a veritable landslide. It couldn't miss a man and horse crossing that ravine. Nor could he turn back. The trail leading down into the cut was edged on one side with a sheer drop, on the other with a steep, blank wall. It was less than a foot and a half wide.

Stuart halted at the point beyond which he could not turn back. He peered up at the head of the ravine, searching for some small movement. He saw nothing, heard nothing. But he couldn't help the strong feeling of uneasiness that gripped him.

How long ago had Ernie passed this way? How badly did he want to destroy Stuart, who he must have known would come after him?

These were questions for which Stuart had no answers. And he couldn't hesitate here forever. If Ernie wasn't waiting up there, he was putting miles between Stuart and himself. He was gaining time—time that Stuart might never make up.

Decisively, then, Stuart put his horse onto the narrow trail and started across. He spurred savagely, recklessly, and his horse plunged fearfully ahead.

Slipping, sliding, lunging and sometimes almost crouching on trembling legs, the horse ran forward along the trail. The led horse pulled back against the reins in Stuart's hand. Stuart looped them quickly around the saddle horn, but the pull of the balky horse against them snapped them like twine.

Freed of the backward pull, Stuart's horse almost fell. But he recovered and plunged ahead, toward the ravine now less than fifty yards away.

And Stuart heard it then. From above came a sharp crack, followed by a deep, throaty rumbling.

He flung a glance overhead. He saw a rubble of rocks rolling down the ravine, saw Ernie standing in the rising dust of their passage, legs spread, hands on hips. Ernie's head was thrown back and Stuart knew he was laughing.

His spurs raked the scrambling horse he rode, and his voice raised in a high, involuntary yell. The horse lunged ahead, but the rocks were traveling now with terrifying speed, crashing down into the ravine, bounding high after the impact, only to fall again with other rocks they had dislodged.

For an instant it looked as though Stuart might make it. Then a rock that had struck the opposite wall, rebounded directly toward him.

He saw it would hit, and knew the bitter taste of defeat. He lay low on his horse's withers and waited.

The boulder, weighing three or four hundred pounds, smashed into the horse's hindquarters.

The impact bowled the horse off the edge, sent him hurtling into empty space. The horse screamed like a stricken woman, and the scream diminished and wavered with his falling, end-over-end movement. He struck the talus slide a hundred and fifty feet below, and from there started a new slide with his rolling, broken body.

Stuart had been flung from the saddle like a doll. He struck the wall and bounced. Then he fell, his upper body on the trail, his legs dangling over the edge. Slowly, slowly, he began to slip, the weight of his legs pulling him toward the drop.

Back on the other side of the gully, the sheriff's horse reared in utter terror, tried to turn and found that he could not. He stood there trembling, staring at Stuart with wild fearful eyes.

CHAPTER NINETEEN

Stuart came to slowly. His first realization was that he was slipping slowly over the edge. His second was that Ernie Post still waited up above, a rifle in his hands. If Stuart moved—if he showed any sign of life—Ernie would put a bullet in his back.

He didn't move. But his body, previously inert, was now taut with muscle as he used his hands to counteract its slipping motion toward the edge.

He breathed shallowly, hoping Ernie was far enough away so that he couldn't see the slight rhythmic pulsation of his body. And he waited.

Seconds ran on into minutes. Still the sheriff's horse stood trembling on the far side of the ravine. The terror had faded from his eyes, to be replaced by a kind of apathy. If left there indefinitely, he would eventually either back along the trail or continue forward and pick his way across the slide. If he backed away, he'd run for town as soon as he was able to get turned around, leaving Stuart here afoot. But if he came this way, Stuart could catch him and mount, provided of course that Ernie had gone on by then.

Voices lifted from down below. The posse was coming. They had left Nora's house and begun the climb toward the rimrock trail. Stuart wished he knew whether Dan had talked to them or not. It might make all the difference in the world.

He waited. Flies droned in the still air. The thunder of the slide had long since died below, but occasionally a loosened pebble came free and bounced along in its wake. Dust, raised by the slide, continued to settle through the air.

Ten minutes had passed since Stuart was thrown from his horse. Ten minutes. Would Ernie wait that long?

Stuart forced himself to wait what he judged was another five. His shoulders ached from the strain. If he didn't climb back on the trail soon he wouldn't get back at all. His muscles would simply refuse to lift his body and he'd slide off to his death against the rocks below.

He tightened his shoulder muscles and edged himself up a couple of inches. He stopped and waited, holding his breath. No shot came from above.

He inched up a little farther and with a final, frantic burst of strength, flung himself full length along the narrow trail.

Still no shots. He sat up and stared up at the place he had seen Ernie last. Ernie was gone.

Stuart stood up. His knees trembled as he looked down at the broken body of his horse. He glanced up again. Then, slowly and carefully, speaking soothing words, he crossed the rocky ravine to the sheriff's horse.

He cut the saddle strings and spliced them to the

broken reins. Then he led the animal across the ravine to the solid trail beyond. It was too narrow here to mount, and both he and the horse were too shaken for that anyway. So he led the horse all the way to the top.

With the shelf trail behind, he heaved a long, slow sigh of relief. Then began to search for Ernie's tracks.

Apparently Ernie had caught a Skull horse on the mountain and led it down for the specific purpose of carrying someone away. Maybe he'd meant to take Nora. Maybe he'd changed his mind. In any event, he now had Katie tied securely on that horse. Probably gagged, too, so she couldn't scream. Otherwise nothing could have kept her quiet while Ernie waited for Stuart to climb the trail.

Their trail was plain, and obviously Ernie was traveling fast. Stuart made a rueful grin that didn't extend to his eyes. The posse. Whether they knew it or not, the possemen had saved his life today. Hearing their voices at the foot of the trail, Ernie had figured he couldn't afford a longer wait, so he had gone on.

So far, Katie probably hadn't been hurt. As long as Ernie was pressed from behind, he'd have no opportunity to hurt her other than to cuff her around a bit. So it was up to Stuart to keep pressing, crowding, to keep Ernie on the run until he got tired of running and stopped to make a stand.

Stuart's head ached excruciatingly. There was a knot on it nearly as big as an egg. When he thought of how close that had been . . .

Ernie's trail, along with that of the led horse, angled

up over the first ridge of the plateau, which appeared flat from below, but wasn't. Then they dropped into a pocket of aspen, and down toward the rim on the far side of this main ridge.

Stuart recognized Ernie's strategy. He was going to force pursuers to proceed strictly by trail, and eliminate the chance of their being able to follow him by sight. It would slow down the pursuit, for not even the most experienced tracker can follow trail as fast as it is made.

Stuart didn't push too hard. The ground beneath the aspen trees was covered with dead leaves, through which the grass had pushed. Not the easiest ground on which to track. And if he lost them, he'd forfeit perhaps half an hour picking up their trail again.

The trail went all the way to the rim, and after that continued in necessarily winding fashion to allow for the irregularities of the rim itself. Here, tracking was even more difficult than it had been back in the aspen thicket, for a six inch carpet of dry spruce needles covered the ground.

Frowning with concentration, Stuart rode on. The miles dropped behind. Whenever he crested a ridge, however small, he looked ahead hopefully. But never once did he sight his quarry.

He was losing ground, and knew it, and the knowledge put the coldest kind of fear into his heart. He had to catch up with Ernie today. He couldn't track in the dark. Ernie would get ahead, even if he only traveled part of the night.

And when he stopped—that was the time of greatest

danger to Katie. Ernie may have thought he had succeeded in killing Stuart. But he'd heard the posse coming up the trail. He would know they couldn't be very far behind.

So he would want to rid himself of Katie, and through her death, exact his revenge against Nora.

Stuart shivered, despite the heat of the mid-morning sun. He began to hurry, though it was against his better judgment.

All the while, he had been puzzling over the direction of the trail, trying to read Ernie's mind, trying to guess his ultimate destination. So far he hadn't been able to. The trail seemed aimless, as though Ernie were only trying to kill the daylight hours without being caught.

Stuart began to remember things about Ernie—his senseless cruelties, the things he had done to animals as a boy. A sense of almost panicked urgency began to creep over him. If he didn't catch Ernie before dark fell, he might find Katie's body in the morning.

Somehow he had to gain back the time he was losing. And yet, how could he, without knowing Ernie's goal?

The sun climbed inexorably to the top of the sky and began to slide down it toward the west. The trail went on and on, twisting, turning, never straightening out long enough to tell Stuart anything.

Perhaps its very vagueness concealed deliberate direction. Perhaps Ernie was planning his course so that when night came down he would be at a certain, specific place.

Ernie relished his cruelties. He dragged them out. So

he would want a place, within four walls, where he could enjoy killing Katie to the fullest.

Winding around this way and never doubling back or coming within sight of trail he had previously made must have a purpose. It must!

Where would Ernie go? Where would he end up as the last light faded from the sky?

There were a number of cabins here on the mountain top, cabins that Stuart knew but members of the posse didn't. Perhaps that was why Ernie had waited there at the head of the trail, so determined to kill Stuart. Perhaps he intended to use one of those cabins tonight and didn't want Stuart alive because he just might guess which one.

Hope began to stir in Stuart's heart. If he *could* guess, and guess right, then he might abandon this slavish following of the trail. He could head directly toward Ernie's hideout cabin and either beat him here or arrive before Katie got hurt.

But which one?

Ernie's trail was circling in its zig-zag way, gradually tending toward the west. Stuart dismounted and examined the tracks of Ernie's horse. He was no novice at reading tracks. These were about two hours old.

That was the time he had lost so far. Enough to doom Katie. Enough to make him fail. He *had* to figure it out. *Now*.

Deliberately he knelt to the ground. He drew a rough map on a bare place, a map of the plateau top. He put an X at his present location.

Next, he carefully retraced the route he had followed

from the time he had climbed the rim. It made a crescent, a semicircle.

Excitement touched him. With his twig, he drew a tentative course beyond this spot, following the same, semicircular curvature as the trail already made.

He frowned with concentration, trying to remember from this crude map on the ground what the land ahead was like. He squinted up at the sun. Mid-afternoon. Three o'clock maybe. Nearly five hours to go until sundown—four and a half at least. Ernie and Katie were traveling at a rate of something like five miles an hour.

Twenty, twenty-five miles along that gentle curve would bring them to the edge of the tall rim, beyond Salt Wash, at the edge of a drainage know as Cottonwood Creek. It was off Skull range, beyond it by several miles. But there *was* a cabin . . .

Stuart checked his map. Excitement kept rising in him. He fought it down, for he could afford no mistakes. He had only this chance, this one chance. If he guessed wrong, or if Ernie was too sly, that ended it.

Yet why would Ernie be trying to outguess anyone? He thought Stuart was dead. As far as he knew, only the posse from town was on his trail.

Stuart tried to remember that cabin, to separate it from the dozen or so others atop the plateau. In his whole life he had been to that cabin less than half a dozen times. It was built of logs, he remembered, with the back wall wholly buried in the hillside for warmth.

Roofed with sod, it contained but a single room. It hadn't been used for years, but nobody had ever destroyed it because it offered shelter from the savage storms that came roaring out of Utah in the winter time. Leaving the cabin might save some solitary rider's life.

Stuart stood up and destroyed the map with his boot toe. He scowled fiercely with indecision. If he went on this way he would arrive too late. But to gamble with Katie's life . . .

He stepped into the saddle. Then, knowing it had to be this or nothing at all, he lifted his horse to a gallop, heading straight across the wide plateau toward the cabin on Cottonwood Creek.

Heading there direct, he could make it well before sundown, probably ahead of Ernie. He could be waiting. He could be sure that Ernie would have no chance to hurt Katie.

The plateau stretched ahead of him endlessly, like a vast prairie. Grouse and sage chickens flew from his path. Occasionally, riding through timber, he startled browsing deer, or a grub-eating bear.

Off to the west, he caught an occasional glimpse of the Utah desert, shimmering with heat, vague with haze and dust. Behind him to the east, the high peaks of the continental divide were lost from sight in blue distance.

The sun inched toward the horizon. Its heat diminished slowly. Shadows lengthened, and the sun's light became less white, picking up various shades of gold and orange.

Stuart came to the fence, pulled it loose from several posts, then stood on the wires while he led his horse across. Without bothering to replace the staples, he rode on.

Fear kept gnawing at him. He would get to the cabin on Cottonwood Creek. He would stay there, waiting, ready . . . and Ernie wouldn't come.

And yet, beneath his fear and uncertainty, he knew that he had done the only thing he could do. The rest was in the hands of fate.

CHAPTER TWENTY

At sundown, Stuart rode into sight of the decaying cabin on the rim above Cottonwood Creek.

It was situated in a draw, just above a spring that seeped out of a pile of shaly rocks. On both sides of the draw, beyond the small clearing surrounding the spring, spruce and aspen combined to form a fair stand of timber.

The cabin itself had changed little. The back wall was still securely buried in the hillside. Weeds grew in profusion from the sod roof. The front wall seemed solid.

Cattle apparently used this spring heavily, for the grass was completely gone within a distance of half a mile of it, and the ground was heavily tracked.

Below the cabin, the draw became steeper as it tumbled away toward the precipitous rim a quarter mile away. Here the water from the spring, grown to a foot-wide stream, cascaded off the rim in a waterfall a thousand feet high.

Stuart tied his horse in the timber. He found a spot

from which he could watch all the approaches to the cabin, and sat down to wait.

He tried not to think. The minutes dragged. Light faded slowly from the sky, leaving the world a desolate gray. And even this gray deepened, until the cabin was little more than a blob of blackness against the lighter shade of the surrounding clearing.

Stuart slipped his gun from its holster, and by feel checked its loads. Absently he fingered the cartridges in his belt. Then he got up and moved closer to the cabin.

With each passing minute, his apprehension increased. He *had* guessed wrong. Ernie had outfoxed him. And tonight Katie Dykes would die at Ernie's hands.

He shook himself angrily. He promised himself that if that did happen, there was no place on earth Ernie could hide from him. He'd find him and when he did . . .

A snapping twig in the timber above the cabin yanked his head around. He froze, listening.

A deer? A shambling, wandering bear? Or a horse?

He waited. He began to sweat, in the night's cool chill. Nerves jumped in his arms and legs.

More plainly, closer, he heard it again.

Noiseless as an Indian, he eased up closer to the cabin. His eyes were narrowed, intent.

Then, with intense relief, he saw the indistinct shapes of two horses move out of the timber and approach the cabin. He'd been right after all. Ernie was here, and so was Katie Dykes.

He started to lunge forward, then checked himself

with an effort. Ernie was a formidable adversary. Physically, Stuart was no match for him.

Nor could he shoot with any degree of accuracy in this light. He couldn't even see his sights.

This was no time to take chances. Not with Ernie, whose cruelties had so often turned him sick with disgust. Not with the man who had knifed Milo in his sleep, who had kidnapped Katie with the express purpose of killing her, slowly and with the excruciating cruelty he enjoyed so much.

There must be no mistakes. Ernie had to die. Stuart had to win this battle, if he never won another.

He told himself that if he had more light he would shoot Ernie down like a wolf. Approaching on stealthy, silent feet, he didn't honestly know whether he could have done that or not. Nor did it matter. What did matter was the fact that the light had faded until he couldn't see to shoot.

He was within a hundred yards of the cabin now, still hidden by shadow. Ernie didn't speak. Big, hulking, he swung to the ground and tied both horses to the rotting rail before the shack. Then he approached Katie, tied and gagged upon her horse.

A gentle wind blew toward Stuart from the pair. And suddenly the unexpected happened, the unforseen thing Stuart both dreaded and feared. The breeze carried to Stuart's horse, tied back in the timber, the scent of these horses in front of the cabin. He nickered, and nickered again.

Ernie moved like lightning for so big a man. He snatched Katie from her saddle, reached the door in a couple of strides and flung her bodily through it. He whirled, stepped aside, and lost himself in the shadows that hid the cabin walls.

Stuart cursed inaudibly as the horse nickered again. After that, complete silence settled over the clearing, silence that stretched away into several minutes.

Stuart strained his ears, trying to hear movement over there. He heard nothing.

He wanted to move in, seek Ernie out, and come to grips with him. He forced himself to remain still. Let Ernie make the first move. Let Ernie expose himself. Katie was safe for now, driven from Ernie's mind by the threat outside.

She must be wild with terror. Ernie would have told her what he intended to do, perhaps in detail. Part of his pleasure would come from Katie's terror.

Nausea crawled in Stuart's stomach. Still he didn't move.

Then, shattering the quiet of the night, he heard Ernie's angry shout, "Who the hell's there? Come on out, damn you, before I cut you down!"

Movement at last over there—a shadowy shape appearing from the shelter of the cabin wall. If only Ernie had arrived sooner! If only there were more light!

But there were sounds—sounds inside the cabin— and this puzzled Stuart. He had thought Katie would be too terrified to move. But she was moving. He could hear her stumbling around inside, knocking things over, as though she had completely lost her mind. A tin can crashed against the stove . . .

And suddenly he understood, for the doorway of the cabin was outlined with light from inside. Katie had been searching for matches. Even with her hands tied, she had found some and struck one . . .

The light grew as trash into which she had dropped the match flared up. Thank God Ernie hadn't tied her feet, and that terror had not completely numbed her mind.

The firelight silhouetted Ernie's body briefly. Stuart leaped into the open, raised his gun and fired.

Ernie's gun flared back almost instantaneously, and then he lunged away, trying to escape the faintly flickering light. He limped, and Stuart knew he'd scored a hit. He stepped closer. He raised his gun, sighting carefully this time, and fired again.

Ernie went down. The fire was growing stronger inside the cabin. It threw more light out the door into the clearing. Katie would be burned! Stuart holstered his gun and raced for the door.

He plunged inside, fumbling in his pocket for his knife. Katie had stumbled and fallen. Too exhausted to get up, she lay squirming on the packed dirt floor. A pile of dry grass and weeds, deposited in the cabin by the wind, blazed furiously over against the wall.

Stuart stooped, slashed the leather bindings on her wrists. He yanked the gag out of her mouth and lifted her up.

Her eyes were flat with terror, her face strained with the unrelieved tension of fear. He wasn't even sure she recognized him. Her voice was cracked and strange. "He's there—out there!"

Stuart said, "He's dead," and carried her toward the door.

Outside, a gun boomed. The bullet slashed along the side of Stuart's neck, bringing an instant rush of blood.

He leaped aside, to the protection of the wall. Smoke was stifling now inside the shack. The heat was almost unbearable.

Stuart laid Katie on the floor. "Stay down here," he said. "The air's better and it's cooler."

He hadn't much time—certainly not enough to play a waiting game. Ernie could wait for Stuart to show himself, but Stuart couldn't wait at all. Heat and smoke were building up too fast inside the shack. It was only a question of time until the brush that supported the sod roof caught. Maybe they wouldn't burn to death. But they'd die for lack of air.

Katie was already weak from her day-long ordeal of fear.

So he had to go outside. That, or die here waiting for Ernie Post to die. God, the vitality of the brute, to recover so quickly from that wound. Stuart knew where his bullet had hit—squarely in the chest. Ernie must be bleeding profusely.

But he could shoot, and somehow he would stay conscious until the fire drove them out. Ernie wouldn't die until Stuart was dead, and Katie too. He would put his monstrous twisted will to that . . .

Katie began to cough. Spasms shook her body as she gasped for air.

Stuart plunged for the door.

He burst through it, running, throwing himself to

one side. Out there in the clearing, illuminated by the flickering light from the fire inside the cabin, Ernie stood. His shirt front was a mass of blood. His face was twisted and beaded with sweat from the tremendous effort of will it took to keep him on his feet. His legs were spread and he looked like a giant standing there.

His gun flared, its muzzle inexorably following Stuart's rapid, falling movement. Ernie had shot a thousand times at a running deer and this was almost the same thing.

The bullet struck Stuart's left spur, tore it loose and flung it against the cabin wall, where it clanged dully. The blow numbed Stuart's foot and leg all the way to the knee. Then he was rolling in the dirt, rolling into the darkness while bullets probed blindly along the course Ernie guessed that he would take.

Two thudded into the cabin wall less than a foot from his head. A third showered him with dirt.

He stopped rolling. He brought his own gun to bear and fired. Immediately he scrambled away without waiting to see if the bullet took effect.

Ernie stood still out there, calmly reloading his gun. Stuart raised his own.

How many bullets did it take to kill this man? A chill of horror touched Stuart's spine as he saw blood begin to well from Ernie's thigh, soaking his pants beneath the wound.

Ernie's gun rose. Stuart looked straight into the bore and knew that this time Ernie would get him. Ernie was waiting for the muzzle flash of Stuart's gun.

When he saw it, he would correct his aim and fire instantly.

It was a chance Stuart would have to take. But taking it, he would kill this giant and put him down for good.

He raised his gun and centered it on Ernie's head. He fired, and saw Ernie's head snap back.

Ernie's gun blasted, scarcely deflected even though he was dead as he squeezed the trigger off.

Stuart waited for the shock of the bullet. When it didn't come, he felt weakness flow through his body like water. He staggered into the cabin, seized Katie and dragged her out.

Katie was weeping, her body shaking hysterically. Stuart tipped up her face and kissed her on the mouth.

"We'll forget all this," he said. "We'll start right now."

"Yes, Stuart."

He helped her away into the timber where his horse stood tied. He lifted her to the saddle and swung up behind. He rode back in the direction he had come, with Katie comfortably warm and oddly silent against his chest.

Before half an hour passed, he heard the clatter of hoofs as the posse rode toward him through the dark.

They had camped for the night, he supposed, but had come on again when they heard the shots and saw the glow in the sky above the burning cabin.

He wished he knew whether Dan Mountain had regained consciousness before the posse left Nora's house. But now, regardless, he had to surrender himself and if necessary go to trial.

He hailed them from the darkness, and immediately heard Vince Doyle's startled bellow, "Hell, it's Stuart Post!" and the shouted query, "Did you catch Ernie? Is Katie all right?"

Stuart rode toward them, still not sure. "She's here with me. Hold your fire."

Doyle yelled back, "It's all right! The sheriff told us what happened! The one he wants is Ernie!"

Stuart approached the shadowy group and halted before them. "Ernie's dead. You'll find him in front of that cabin at the head of Cottonwood Creek."

After a brief discussion, the others went on, but Doyle hung back. "I got a lot to make up for, Stu. That beating and all."

"It's over now," Stuart said wearily.

"Yeah. I—"

"You'll get water and you'll get grass," Stuart said. "You'll get paid for your cattle too." His voice was almost curt. He couldn't stir up much of a friendly feeling toward Doyle. Not yet.

Doyle mumbled, "Thanks Stu. Thanks," and galloped after the others. After that the night was still, except for the night noises of the animals and birds that inhabited it.

He swung his horse, rode down a draw into a grove of fragrant aspens, halted and lifted Katie to the ground. He held her close against him.

Tomorrow they would go back to Skull, but tonight was theirs, here under the peaceful, silent stars. And tonight would be all the sweeter for the violence that had gone before.

Center Point Publishing
600 Brooks Road ● PO Box 1
Thorndike ME 04986-0001 USA

(207) 568-3717

US & Canada:
1 800 929-9108